HATCHED

Celebrating 20 years of the
Tim Winton Award for Young Writers

FREMANTLE PRESS

in association with

CITY OF
SUBIACO

This anthology brings together
the winners of the
Tim Winton Award for Young Writers
from 1993 to 2012.

Contents

Foreword
TIM WINTON

It's an odd thing to have a writing award given in your name, especially when you're not dead yet. But clearly, not being dead has its rewards. The pay-off is being here to see young people exercising their hearts and minds for the pleasure and excitement of simply being allowed to do so. And if being the patron of such a prize is premature then I'll just have to endure it as another form of being a little early and a bit awkward, as is my lifelong habit.

I have been a professional storyteller all my adult life. I grew up hearing stories told by my parents and grandparents and I caught the bug early. Books were always a part of my life but before books there were the tall tales and true that I heard at the dinner table (and sometimes under the dinner table) at ordinary meals or special occasions when the rellies got together. I was a child of the television age. I grew up reading comic books and listening to rock and roll. I knew, as every child does, that old people are strange and boring and best avoided.

But when hairy-eared great-uncles got warmed up with a bellyful of food and a bit of winter sunshine they'd say things that caught my attention. Their opinions were of no account at all, but their stories were something else. They always had their origins in events that had happened to them — complicated, embarrassing, terrifying, hilarious incidents — stories with twists and turns, sudden reversals, narrow escapes and unlikely endings. Other relatives had variations on the same stories, corrections or elaborations, sometimes entirely different versions of the same event. Many of these tales had been honed over many decades, smoothed and sprung by many tellings. And when now and then I had the creeping sense that a story was not strictly true it didn't matter a bit. If it was a good tale well told, so much the better. A great story rescued many a dreary family gathering.

I liked the way some family tales became reports from an alien world, a different life altogether. My grandparents grew up in the horse and cart era and died in the computer age. Without their stories they would have been very strange and distant people to a boy like me who saw men walk on the moon at age nine. Stories brought us together. They were an important part of the family fabric.

Storytelling is a deep human impulse. We've been doing it since people began carving bones and sticks and daubing the walls of caves. You can hear it in ancient songs and poems and of course it's there in all forms of writing. Every culture, every family is held together by story. Humans will always need to record their experiences, to mull them over, to wonder what all these events and portents mean. At its core a story is essentially saying, 'I was here; this happened to me'. We tell stories to celebrate life, to warn each other of physical or moral danger, or simply to make something beautiful and symmetrical from a life that is often ugly and chaotic. When we seem to be surrounded by an excess of mere information, stories often cut through and live in the memory.

It's a great pleasure to see young people exercising their storytelling instincts. During the twenty years in which the award has been given in my name I've had the privilege of witnessing this stubborn, lovely impulse as it lives on in a new generation. Whether they're writing feverish fantasy or gritty realism these young writers are coming to terms with their language and their lives, using stories to shape or unpack what they know and what they fear and what they hope for. In my mind the award has never been about identifying and rewarding the great writers of the future, though it may well do that over time in its small way. For me the chief purpose is to glory in storytelling, to give the impulse space in which to flourish, to celebrate this important part of human life. My hope is that by creating a positive environment in which young people can exercise their imagination and test their linguistic skills their lives and minds will be enlarged. There is no empathy without imagination. Civilised life requires enormous imaginative effort, for how else can we live a civil, moral existence unless we empathise with others and imagine what their lives and problems and dreams might be?

When this enterprise began, thanks to the staff of the Subiaco Library, I was the father of young children. Nowadays I'm a grandfather. I've met previous award winners who are now parents themselves. Many former young writers have gone on to completely unrelated fields. If this award does no more than help produce a few large-hearted accountants and the occasional astronaut with a taste for words as much as data, then it will have made a worthy contribution. My hope is it leaves a few fond memories of childhood and youth and perhaps a tall tale or two. In the meantime it's great to see young people excited and rewarded for doing something as pointless and beautiful as telling stories.

I'm very proud to have been associated with this community-building award and to see all these hearts and minds at work and play. We have their stories. We know they were here. And this is just the beginning. They have so much ahead of them.

Tim Winton

2012

The Broccoli Tree
MERRY LI

Presbyterian Ladies' College
upper secondary category

The $9.99 all-you-can-eat buffet is on the tenth floor of an ageing hotel. Midday sunlight from the lone window projects stripes of light from the knives and forks onto the ceiling, while the fluorescent lighting carves strange pockets of shadow on the tables and plates. Inside, a group of old men congregate around two tables pushed together for their weekly prostate cancer support session. Next to the window, a family of tourists eat dessert, killing an hour before the shuttle bus to the airport is due to arrive. Barry sits at the table next to them, watching the mother pluck the cherry off the mocked cream on her cake and hand it to her youngest daughter. He smiles at them, leans over and says, 'You have a beautiful daughter.' The mother gives him one of those pursed-lip smiles favoured by security guards and thirty-year-old women, and awkwardly shuffles her seat closer to her daughter's. 'Oh, thank you.' He smiles back anyway, and turns to the daughter. 'You should try the black forest cake. It's lovely.'

It's Saturday morning and Barry checks his mobile phone for new messages. It is out-dated now, once resplendent in its mirror-finish flip-top glory. There are three messages, all from various real estate agencies. 'Hi, this is just to let you know that a property near you, 4/31 Regent Street recently sold for $235,000. Call us at any time to discuss your property needs and receive a free valuation. Russel & Russel Real Estate.' He deletes this one and scrolls down. 'Hi Mr Smith, thought you might be interested in viewing 7 Franklin Crescent, open for inspection today 12 pm — 12:30 pm. Auction on site Saturday week. Regards, Brian.' He takes out the street directory that he keeps in the drawer next to the Gideon and looks for Franklin Crescent in the index. It is not far away, two streets past the milk bar. The third message informs him that it is his last chance to pre-purchase a new apartment at an early bird rate. He deletes this one as well and goes to the minibar fridge to retrieve his milk. The cleaning lady, Greta, has wedged the 500 mL carton in the door shelf, next to the Perrier water dated 2003. Barry picks it up and notices that she has folded the flaps over and clipped them with a paperclip. God bless her. He hopes she will stay and chat when she comes to change the sheets and verify that the Perrier remains untouched. Often she rattles on about the new schedule that they have to stick to now that a third of the housekeeping staff have been made redundant. Sixteen bloody rooms a shift, eight before lunch and eight after. Sometimes she will tell him about her children. Robbie's still up at the mines and Rachel's decided to study fashion design at TAFE now. Hopefully she'll stick at it longer than half a semester. Always flitting about, that girl. Greta doesn't understand why Barry is still here. 'It's been — how long? — almost a year now, hasn't it? Still no luck with the house hunting?' She used to ask him about the cheese in the fridge and the kettle appropriated for soup making, told him that he should buy some fruit for the vitamins, but now she just dusts around the cup-a-soup box atop the TV. He doesn't tell her that he has no interest in buying any of the houses he inspects.

I take off my shoes and the real estate agent hands me a clipboard and a pen. I dutifully fill out my contact

details and she points me down the hallway to the
kitchen. They have one of those arty IKEA fruit bowls
made of twisted wires. Bananas in a bird's nest. I have
made it a personal rule that I do not touch anything. I
don't turn things over; I walk around with my hands
in my pockets. Their telephone hangs on the wall
above the kitchen bench. Next to it they keep one of
those memo pads emblazoned with real estate agency
logos that are dropped in letterboxes periodically. Mr
Russel of Russel & Russel has had his eyeballs poked
out with a ballpoint pen. It is these strange little
details that I enjoy on Saturday mornings; it always
surprises me how much you can notice without even
touching a thing. On the fridge there is a cat calendar,
held up on two corners with an Eiffel Tower magnet
and a Seaworld dolphin. Thursdays are labelled with
'Matt: soccer' and alternate Fridays with 'Aunt Thelma
doctor 3 pm'. February 14 is circled for some reason,
and it is not until I am in the garden that I realise it is
Valentine's Day. Outside the lawn has just been mown,
the yellow roots of the grass are showing through, pale
tan lines under the high sun.

Barry arrives early on Sunday morning and stands
outside the church, waiting for the service to finish.
The air is thick and foggy, like a smoker's breath from

one of those government ads. He goes to the church across the road each week, not for the service but for the church group that convenes afterwards, with meetings often stretching out until lunchtime. Today they are holding a thrift sale. He sees two boxes of children's toys left under a tree, and goes to retrieve them. The cardboard is pockmarked with rain, and the sides like soggy Weet-Bix. He takes the toys out and places them under the veranda to dry, pouring the water out of a Tonka truck. When the rain has been squeezed out of all the dolls' hair, they are onto their last hymn. Barry likes being early. He has realised that it is during those little snippets of time at the start and end of things that people tend to divulge a little about their lives. The last strains of the organ hang in the air as the doors open and Carol walks down the steps. 'Barry! How was your week?'

'Yeah, not too bad. How was yours?'

'Oh, an absolute shocker ...' She hands him a box of tablecloths and they begin to set up.

It is late afternoon now, and the sky buckles and folds as I lock up this place. Thirty-five years spent elbow-deep in flour and water. I used to sit here on these stone steps each afternoon, scraping out the semi-dried dough from underneath my fingernails, a sack of unsold bread at my side. As I put the key into an envelope I find myself thinking of boarding school, when I was a boy in suspenders and a woollen cap. They told me of this idea of limbo during the R.E. classes. It was technically the first circle of hell but I saw it as this in-between place, halfway between heaven and hell, a waiting room, if you will — an eternal waiting room for those who were neither sinners nor saints. All these years I have found it strangely comforting that we had not been forgotten, all the ordinary people who were not evil enough to warrant an eternal stay in the fiery pits of hell, but not nearly virtuous enough for the spoils of heaven. I walk home through the old part of town, and I wonder what I have done with the last fifty years.

The thrift sale goes well, lasting until mid-afternoon. They sort the unsold items into various piles and pack them into boxes. One of the ladies brings out a plate of cakes, and another goes to make tea. They sit around the folding tables and talk about their husbands, their children, their irregular menstrual cycles. Afternoon turns to evening and the talk turns to dinner. They thank Barry for his help as he loads the folding table into the boot of someone's car. It is still early, the sun still at eye level, so Barry decides to stop at the milk bar on the way back. He weaves his way through the queue of cars waiting for petrol and crosses over to the sliding doors. There is a two-for-one deal on tuna snack packs so he buys four to keep in the fridge. He rings the bell at the counter and a student emerges clutching a physics textbook. She drops it face down on the counter and rings up his purchases. '$5.20 please.' Back in the hotel, they are changing the prices on the sign for dinner. There are only two customers, but a waiter comes and points him to the corner table wordlessly. He seats himself next to one of the businessmen instead. That way, he can say he's here on business too. He can ask him what he thinks of the city. It usually works, never once has he been asked what his business is. They are carrying out the soup tureens now, a man on each handle. Barry lifts the lid on one of them, cream of chicken. Most of the chicken pieces have been desecrated, the rest of it is drowning broccoli.

I am back at our old house, the one with the swing set and the long grass. It is time for the early news on TV, which my mother has turned on, and now she is pouring sauce onto the broccoli. 'Barry! Dinner!' There is not enough sun left to properly cook my mud pies, and the concrete barely retains the afternoon heat, so I tip the mud into the gutter and go inside. I feel my mother's wedding ring cold against my back as she steers me into the kitchen. I don't know why she still wears it; it's been a long time in my four-year-old mind. She lifts me onto the step stool under the sink, and turns on the tap. Her hands cover mine in a swathe of lemony soap, and I watch the splattered drops of water darken on my t-shirt as we rinse our hands. Dinner is lamb and broccoli. I eat the lamb and leave the broccoli. My mother watches, and begins to tell me a story about the tree across the street. Even now, I have no idea what kind of tree it was, and I suspect it was one of the ageing paperbarks that littered our suburb. I had always thought that it resembled a slightly dehydrated piece of broccoli — a thick flaking trunk and a head of green tufts. Piece by piece, the broccoli leaves my plate.

Orwell's Children
MICHELLE AITKEN

John Curtin College of the Arts
lower secondary category

The bell rings and a slow murmur blossoms inside the school building. Feet knead crowded floors, books are collected and chatter echoes and intensifies. The doors are opened, and a smooth gradient of students snakes away. Black through to white, short through to tall, first the plus then the minus rationed factions break away to board Transqualisers, designed to take everyone home, and all arrive at the same time. Two individuals with female secondary sex characteristics flash their ID chips across the tag station, under the quiet gaze of the bored, bespectacled, brow of the driver. He peers over a heavy tome, *The Able Transqualiser Driver*, open to a page on the practical application of quantum mechanics in space, at an overhead display, showing their Plus10 transport time rationing codes, and they head toward the back of the Transqualiser.

'Hey Tiggy?' whispers the shorter, less attractive, and less intelligent of the two, 'I got 100% on our test!'

Tiggy smiles. 'Well done, Pea, so did I.'

Her pale, slender pianist's fingers rub her left forearm, where she knows her rationing chip is implanted. Tall, smart, athletic, Tiggy is rationed as a Minus50. Her physical, mental, and sensory abilities, as well as her genetic assay and background, entitle her to be marked down, and disadvantaged in the name of equality control.

'150% — 50 rationing points, of course I did,' Tiggy mutters, and when Pea smiles quizzically, apologetically tapping her pink ear, 'I was just saying how nice it is that we are all the same,' was Tiggy's cautious reply. 'Your 50% and Plus50 rationing points makes everything so simple and fair.' The pair fall into silence, with the Transqualiser swaying beneath them; Pea relaxed in her Minus50 chair, and Tiggy agilely shifting weight to stay upright in her Plus50 allocated standing space.

Pea is first to break the silence. 'What's wrong,

Tiggy?' she asks, glancing up at the troubled face of her friend.

'Oh, nothing,' is the reply, but before Pea can probe further, she continues in a quiet tone. 'I've been thinking Pea. About fairness.' She pauses and lowers her voice, glancing around at the other people engaged in light hearted conversation. 'What if rationing isn't the way to be fair? It's never been done before in history, and something that really only benefits half of the population.'

'Tiggy!' Pea cuts in, a note of fear in her hushed voice. 'Fair is for everyone. Plus rationed people and Minus rationed people are brought to the same level, so there is no stress, no reputation to uphold, and no leaders, which means complete happiness in equality.' Tiggy's immediate thought is to the lack of direction and bumbling amiability of her peers, but she doesn't reply, and instead lapses into silence. She knows that with the allowed safe history ration, nobody else would be able to see the gap between human potential, and the reality of society. Even thinking of bridging the gap was nauseating to the Minus population, and incomprehensible to their Plus counterparts.

'I've been thinking, Pea Lovely,' Tiggy ventures again, and is quickly shushed by her friend, out of habit. Pea glances around nervously.

'You know we don't have second names, Tiggy! Our dis/adv lineage is mapped at birth, and then we are freed by rationing, to be members of modern society.' Even Pea knew, however, that parroting lines from their social studies textbook would do nothing to steer Tiggy away from the alluring temptation to think too much.

'But people used to have last names!' Pea's feeble attempt at diversion had been completely unheeded.

'Shh!'

'Sometimes they would even change their names!'

'To be better?' Pea looks around, her face scrunched up and her mouth open in displeasure, as though trying to keep the shells of Tiggy's words from shattering the foundations laid in her mind.

'To be better! Sid Vicious! It's fabulous, it just makes you want to —'

'Stop! Stop!' Pea whines dolefully, then clamps her small fingers over her mouth. Tiggy apologises, breathing deeply, her nails cutting into her forearm subconsciously, a habit ingrained from hours of peeling away skin to reach the microchip underneath.

'It's alright Tiggy. But be careful.' Pea sighs, carefully concealing the roots of jealousy, the sick and unusual feeling that someone is better than her. The driver watches them leave the Transqualiser over an article on domestication through genome profiling. The title of the book is *The Able Transqualiser Driver, Vol II*.

The sun filters through shades on the Transqualiser windows, and bleary eyed students sit in fuzzy morning silence on the way to school. The driver puts down his *Transqualiser Driver Monthly*, dog-earing a page on the effects of dams on ecosystems, and starts the engine again. Tiggy glances up at Pea, but before she can say a word, she is violently shushed. 'You better have not been thinking, Tiggy,' Pea hisses vehemently, fear and concern for her friend expressed through frustration. Tiggy drops her eyes again, neither confirming nor denying Pea's suspicions. Instead, she plays idly with the sensation of knowledge, enough to clear the morning fluff away, the OpenAccess InfoKey burning in her pocket. Borrowing Pea's key is no longer enough, as although she is given more access, historical information is not available to students. Tiggy thinks carefully about what to do with the power of unlimited access to the World Wide Web, free from the Plus50 equality control regulation filter that allowed her limited access to balance the distribution of knowledge. The first thing she had done the previous night, after stealing the key from an Equality Control official, was to find out about the world of Rosa Parks. Something about a world where the superior group proclaimed themselves superior, and acted with superiority, enjoying being better than others, seems to her almost as wonderfully fair as the world she lives in. After being taught to watch people rationed above her receive more equality control rations in every aspect of life, and to smile and enjoy the freedom of all being equal, Tiggy needs to get out.

The Transqualiser, illuminated by white light and casting faint silhouettes on the darkening bitumen, heads towards the dorms, filled with echoes of excited chatter about the coming weekend. Tiggy and Pea wait in their now normal silence, the distance between them expanding daily, alongside Tiggy's knowledge of the past, and her desire to reach the rebels. Pea is scared for her friend, whose raw and weeping arm shows her increasingly desperate attempts to remove her microchip, as though somehow that would make it possible for the rebels to find her. Pea thinks back weeks, months, to when Tiggy first heard of the rebels. The old, content, Tiggy had been standing in her same allocated spot on the Transqualiser, as she excitedly told Pea about a society of outcasts who played music and did art and had talent and learning, and competed on sheer merit, without rationing points to make things fair. Pea's expression had been one of the usual exasperation at Tiggy's insistence on questioning fairness, but changed to horror at the thought of a place where people were given the same treatment, no matter their ability or background. Hushed secrecy had begun to surround their discussions, as paranoia about being discovered to have OldKnowledge took over Tiggy's life. From behind a publication wrapped in brown paper and illustrated with graphs concerning the mineral content of the earth's surface, however, the driver had listened attentively.

Tiggy and Pea both watch out of the window, gazing past their reflections to the steady conveyor belt of quaintly identical houses for sale, parading slowly backwards along the Minus20 Street the Transqualiser traverses. 'Thank Equality Control, for the first home-buyer's grant that lets people buy those lovely houses.' Pea ventures timidly.

'Yes, thank Equality Control for the second home-buyers tax, and not to mention the ColourGradient Allowance scheme, and the dis/adv lineage housing entitlement restrictions ...' Tiggy trails off, leaving Pea confused. 'They don't have that stuff with the rebels, you know,' Tiggy tells her friend quietly, receiving a warning glance.

'Equality Control will find out. Tiggy, you have to

stop.' Pea says, her voice wavering, and to her surprise, meets no resistance.

'Give me your seat, Pea!' Tiggy says suddenly, determined but resigned. The Transqualiser lurches to a stop, and the driver walks down towards the back. He swipes Tiggy's forearm with a transmitter, adding a disobedience warning to her rationing data set, and tells Pea to keep her seat. He turns back towards the front, and brushes against Tiggy on the way past, slipping a note into her pocket. The Transqualiser lurches into motion, with nothing to show for the incident but a slightly increased velocity to make up lost time.

'Meet me at your Transqualiser stop tonight. Bring any OldKnowledge, and means of access. I can take you to the rebels.'

2010

The Untouchable
POPPY DAMON

Shenton College
upper secondary category

Unthinkable

There are many things that I've been told are
unthinkable. Murder. Violence. Rape (I'm not entirely
sure what rape is but the news makes it sound
dreadful). But obviously they are thinkable because
people think them. Then do them. So.

On the news the other day I watched an item
that described a man who'd kept his daughter in his
basement for fifteen years. They'd had kids (the dad
and daughter). Those kids had never seen daylight. The
reporter called it an 'unthinkable act'. But I couldn't

help thinking that that just didn't make any sense. Maybe the man didn't think about it when he drugged her. Maybe it didn't cross his mind that it was wrong when he put up wallpaper in the annex where he kept her. Or when he put food through the trap door for their dinner. Every night. For fifteen years. Maybe what the reporter meant was he couldn't have thought about it, and have done it. Maybe he put it in a different box in his head. Like when people are 'absent minded'. Like when I'm talking and I take apart whatever I'm holding; pens, phones, figurines. Maybe it's like that. So that's how the unthinkable act happened, and we on our sofas have to think about it instead. We think about it a lot if you're like me. Dr Phistine says I'm 'easily affected'. But I don't think a man imprisoning his daughter for fifteen years is me being easily affected, I just think about how bad it is. How I'm glad I'm not her.

Untouchable

When I was real little, I used to play a game called Untouchable. It was a bit like Tag except if you got touched you had to act out a really dramatic death that was really gory. You stayed dead until the cure man (usually me) came and healed you. Like Jesus I guess. Although I didn't believe in him then and I don't believe in him now. So.

In India there was a caste system. There still is one kinda today. Some people are real high up like a celebrity and they're the best you can be. Then there are a few mid-range like doctors, then teachers then builders. Then there are 'The Untouchables' that no one notices, or looks at or smells or speaks to or tastes. They're nothing. If you believe that if a tree falls in a forest and no one hears it, it doesn't make a sound. That's philosophy though and I'm not really sure if it isn't just making out how important humans are. Mum used to say it was self indulgent. That people should just get on with life.

When I found all that out about India I used to have dreams where Mum was there. I'd scream. Not in fright. I'd scream so she could hear me. I'd scream as loud as I could. And jump up and down, and rub fish on me and put nettles on my hands. But she wouldn't notice me. It was like she was in a bottle, or underwater or on TV and she couldn't hear me. It'd be like that I guess, if you were an Untouchable in India.

But then I got to thinking. There would be other Untouchables who could touch you. I even asked Dr Phistine and he said I was very perceptive. I thought I was just pointing out the obvious. But it made me think it was stupid to call them Untouchable when they could hug, kiss and smell and taste and stare at each other at least. It'd be like being on the outside with friends. All looking at Mum. She was the true Untouchable then.

Dysfunctional

'My pen is unfunctional.'

'Dysfunctional.'

'Huh?'

'You said: my pen is unfunctional, you meant to say dysfunctional, you used the wrong prefix.'

'I did what?'

'Never mind.'

A dysfunctional family is one that doesn't work. Most of the time people mean unconventional, rarely do they mean dysfunctional. Where the family sit or sleep all day, where it's an empty house or no house because they stop paying bills, or going to work, and everyone's just beings, even the Grand-pop and the kids and the mum and dad. All of them as individuals don't function. Until they die.

If there are problems or you're just not nuclear that's different. Real different. 'Dysfunctional family' is the kind of thing they put on ads for sitcoms.

'Watch everybody's favourite dysfunctional family next Monday, in *All Under the Same Roof!* Right here on SBS.'

Their biggest problem is the dad doesn't like the mother-in-law and the mum isn't a good cook.

But they function. They do it with big smiles.

'I'm unfunctional.'

'What do you mean?'

'I don't sleep, I don't eat, I don't—'

'You do. You're just sad while you do them.'

That's when I saw the difference.

Unspeakable

Here are all the things that I think but don't say:

1. I'm scared I'll be like you.
2. I don't want anyone to touch me and everyone to touch me all at the same time.
3. Please stop looking at me like that. I'm fine.

Here's what I always say:

'I have a toothache.'

Dr Phistine says it's to 'deflect'.

'Why don't you go to school?'

'I have a toothache.'

'You're deflecting'

'Sorry.'

'What do you think of your mum?'

'She had a toothache?'

'You're doing it again.'

'What?'

'Deflecting.'

'Huh?'

Sigh. Raises eyebrows. Clicks pen. Writes something. Sometimes I imagine what he writes down.

> *Deflects. Can't use prefixes correctly. Easily affected by current affairs. Perceptive.*

When I got home I switched on the news man.

'The girl was discovered because of a neighbour invited to the house by Mr Fritzle for a drink. Mr Hurtz said that he didn't notice anything wrong at all, until he noticed a crack in one of the walls. When he peered closer, he saw a glimpse of the imprisoned family. That chance sighting lead to the rescue of Fritzle's daughter who is now thirty years old.'

What makes some things unthinkable and some unspeakable? When can I think 'I want to marry you' and when can I say it? When can I not think 'I hate you'? When can I not speak it? When can I yell so loud my lungs sag because I've used up all the air yelling I hate you?

How do people know what's an unthinkable act and something just really, really bad?

In India they have psychics read your star sign when you're born and decide where you are in the caste. Your parents pray you're not an Untouchable.

(Unless they're Untouchable I guess. Or maybe they'd want a better life for their kids than what they had. Unless they liked being Untouchable because it was like when I wear my sunnies and I'm invisible. But I guess no one would want to be like that all the time.)

Imagine that much power if you were a psychic in India. Imagine if you just didn't go to the meeting, and you didn't know if you were a celebrity or an Untouchable. Imagine if *you* were one thing and your parents another and you lived together but had to be separate. That'd be almost dysfunctional if they couldn't take care of you. That's what parents are supposed to do.

Unthinkable

Last week I switched on the news. Last week I ate. I slept. I just did them all sadly.

Then, today, I did the unthinkable. I went to school. It wasn't so bad I guess. But we treat some people as Untouchables and some like celebrities. I'm not sure how we decide though because as far as I know none of us are psychics.

I keep lists now. Unspeakable. Unthinkable. Untouchable. Dysfunctional. Unconventional. I also keep a 'To-do-list'. On the top of the list is 'smile' next 'live' then 'un-smile', 'sleep'. I've written it over and over. My family's functional, we're just unconventional because we function sadly. Like we're all in separate castes and sometimes I want to rub fish on me and put nettles on my hands and say 'I hate you!' until my lungs sag. But instead I watch the news.

At least I'm not in a cellar. At least Dad didn't forget to think 'don't imprison my daughter'. He can forget other things, like Mum. Just never think the unthinkable. Say the unspeakable. Touch the Untouchables or be dysfunctional. These are the rules. We've followed them for centuries and they've worked pretty well so far, right? So.

Gandhi didn't like the caste system, he thought it was dysfunctional. I did a project on him last week.

He was wrong. It functioned. It functioned for ages. It was just bad for the Untouchables. It worked. It looked good to some, but inside it had cracks.

It was just chance that someone saw them.

Smile. Live. Unsmile. Sleep.

2009

The Piano Man
RACHEL HAO

St Hilda's Anglican School for Girls
lower secondary category

Mrs Across-The-Road peered curiously past her curtain. He was playing again, his back visible through the front lounge window, the scalic, harmonious sounds floating out into the street. The suit he wore was as immaculate as always, his face hidden in the gloomy shadows of the room. The occasional glimpse of his fingers could be seen as they danced along the length of the black and white keys.

Outside, children delirious with freedom after a week of school ran up and down the street, laughing and shouting. Maple leaves fell around them, signalling the autumn to come, although the blue skies above told a different story. But the Piano Man, as Mrs Across-The-Road had come to call him, was oblivious to the children's voices. It was as if the glass of his window *staccato*-ed his world from the world outside. He just continued to play.

Mrs Across-The-Road was a nosy woman. Constantly peeking behind her floral curtains, her elongated neck and pointy nose became her. She knew the scandal between Mr Number 3 and The Around-The-Corners, the due date of Number 24's baby, the secret romance of the Number 13 and Number 15 teens. But she had never been able to understand the Piano Man. He was such a novelty — not so much the music, but more the mystery that surrounded him. She would often peer out her window, looking at the Piano Man's house, on the pretext that she was 'dusting the mantle'. But the only time she ever saw him was when he was in his front lounge, playing his piano.

The Cul-De-Sacs were an average enough family. Father, mother, daughter, son. The son played football, the daughter drew. The father an accountant, the mother a secretary. But behind closed doors, 'normality' disappeared. Father and Mother either ignored each other, or shouted until they turned hoarse, the voices clashing discordantly. Mother had an affair, Father didn't care. The parents had turned their daughter's and son's lives into ones of pretence, as they struggled to keep up the façade of the 'perfect' family.

Son started getting into fights at school, while Daughter totally detached herself from the rest of the world. However, both found solace whenever the Piano Man played. The two teenagers would escape their parents' arguments; Son on the roof, Daughter on the veranda. Neither knew the other was there — instead they lost themselves in the music; allowed themselves a moment of peace in their lives.

Number 16 didn't believe in marriage. He was frequently seen lecturing others about how love didn't benefit anybody in the world. He wouldn't fall in love, no he wouldn't; it would all end in ruin and disaster anyway.

Music wasn't much better, in Mr 16's opinion. It was all just a glorified concept, with the formulaic music of the past and the hip-bip-boppy music of today. And yet that man down the road insisted on banging away on that stupid piano.

It had been a normal day for Mrs Across-The-Road, the day it happened. She had made the kids breakfast, sent them off to school, watched *Oprah*, and looked out her window several times. It wasn't until afternoon, after the kids had eaten their snacks and retreated to their rooms, that she saw the white Ford Anglia with the grey trailer pull up beside the Piano Man's house. Through the window, the Piano Man continued to play, unaware as always to the happenings beyond his fingers and the black and white keys. A man in a baseball cap climbed out of the car, made his way up the path, knocked on the Piano Man's door.

It was the first time anything had ever happened at the Piano Man's residence, and although he was still playing, the man in the cap was beginning to become impatient. Mrs Across-The-Road was sure something about the Piano Man's identity was about to be revealed, and she was there to witness it!

Daughter and Son of the Cul-De-Sacs were also home when the man pulled up at the Piano Man's residence. He was playing Daughter's favourite Chopin prelude when the knocking began. On and on it went, doing nothing for the music. She started to get up, to ask the man to just *go away*, but before she could the music stopped. It was the first time she had seen the Piano Man acknowledge the world beyond his piano. A few moments later, the door opened, and there stood the Piano Man.

There stood the Piano Man, to the son's surprise. He had never seen his face before; he doubted anybody in the neighbourhood had. It was a painfully normal face — one that you could easily pass over in a busy crowd. Dark hair, dark eyes, thin chin. His skin was a shade paler than most, which could be explained by how he never seemed to come out of the house.

'Sir, I'm here representing your benefactors at the FSE. Numerous letters have been sent to your residence about the overdue debt caused by the unfortunate fall of your stocks. I'm afraid if you do not have the money I will have to take some of your belongings to pay off your debts.'

Mr 16 saw that piano playing bloke for the first time on his way home from work that day. He was with a man in a baseball cap, who seemed to be getting quite frustrated actually, almost shouting as the Piano Man just stared blankly back at him.

'Sir ... pay ... repayment ... SIR ... debt ... sir ... instalment ... sir?... listening ... me?'

So Mr 'I-Love-The-Piano-And-Can't-Stop-Playing-It' was in a bit of money trouble? Mr 16 thought gleefully. Finally his comeuppance was here! Strolling confidently towards the two men, Mr 16 lifted his arm in a half wave of acknowledgement towards the Debt Collector.

'What's going on over here? Need any help?'

'Well, is this man foreign or deaf? Because he doesn't seem capable of responding at all to what I say.'

'Yes, he is quite a mystery isn't he? I doubt he has any money for his debts — in fact I think the only thing that could sell would be his piano ...'

Mrs Across-The-Road couldn't believe her eyes! How dare that Number 16 and his baseball capped accomplice take away the piano, with the Piano Man obviously in a state of blank incomprehension? Without his piano, the poor man would disappear into anonymity; lose the thing that made him whole. Mrs Across-The-Road was normally a passive woman, but for once in her life, she felt a sense of conviction. She had to do something!

Son and Daughter of the Cul-De-Sacs met at the path outside their door, both thinking the same thing. To stop the removal of the piano! In a normal situation they may have wondered at the fact that they had both been engrossed in the same thing although both felt so alone — but the pressing issue of the Piano Man muted their voices. Instead they just looked at each other in a split second of acknowledgement, before both rushed out the house; half in anger, half in desperation.

The doorway of the Piano Man's house had never been so crowded. It was bad enough with that woman from across the road lecturing the two grown men like they were her children, her apron still tied tightly around her waist. But then the two teenagers from down the road also came barging in, shouting loudly about 'unfair treatment', amid many swears and curses.

But he didn't care about all the raucous sounds around him; instead his attention was completely focused on the precious instrument that had been abandoned on the pathway. Walking toward it with deliberation, he sat down on the worn seat and slightly adjusted the height. Around him, the arguments continued, the voices growing louder and louder. However, as he raised his hands, his fingers poised above the familiar keys, sound around him grew gradually irrelevant. Instead a haze of calm and anticipation settled over him, as his inner metronome began ticking. *3, and, 4, and ...*

As the music began again, the voices were forced into submission, as notes led into each other, until finally melding together in a thick, perfect harmony. The Debt Collector was at a loss for words; already diminished by the lecture of the woman, this was the final straw. Retreating hastily to his car, he decided that he would no longer do the dirty work of others before making sure there wouldn't be such drama involved.

Mr 16 watched the Debt Collector go sulkily. So much for his master 'Stop The Music' plan. The stupid woman and children had sat down on the porch, gloating at their success. Mr 16 opened his mouth to say something, but the woman glared at him with malice. *Maybe not today,* he thought, as he hurried on his way back to the security of his home at Number 16.

Outside, the joyous notes of Dvorak's ninth symphony cadenza rang through the street, as the man in the suit sat at his piano, and continued to play.

Mrs T's Shoe Collection

AMBERLEY SPARKES

Bertram Primary School
middle primary category

Screech went a rather small green bus as it came to a halt. Mrs T scrambled up from her seat and hobbled past Henry the bus driver.

'Have you been shopping again Mrs T?' questioned Henry.

'Ooh yes Henry, you know I can't stop myself. I just love shopping,' smiled Mrs T.

'Shoes again I bet,' Henry said with a wink.

'There was a shoe sale on today and I couldn't resist them. So I bought lots and lots. All different colours, styles and sizes,' Mrs T happily explained.

'Have a good afternoon then Mrs T. I can't sit here all afternoon talking,' Henry said as he waved goodbye.

Everyone called Mrs Tarvoskinichie Mrs T because Mrs Tarvoskinichie is such a mouthful.

Mrs T hummed her way happily up her garden path slowing down to check her letterbox for any shoe catalogues. After finding none, with a sigh Mrs T continued on her way switching her bags from hand to hand. Mrs T unlocked the door, stepped inside and tripped over some shoes. 'Oh dear,' she said, embarrassing herself as she blushed and turned to see if anybody saw her, then she quickly closed the door.

Mrs T went into the kitchen to have a cup of tea. Mrs T always liked to have a strong cup of tea when she went shoe shopping. Mrs T put the kettle on and went to find a place to put the shoes.

First she went to her wardrobe and saw ... forty-five pairs of shoes all squashed together. 'Ooh I do like shoes,' Mrs T said to herself, as she looked at all different colours, styles and sizes. Mrs T heard the kettle boil so with a sigh she walked slowly to the kitchen and sat down. While Mrs T drank her tea she thought about where to put her new shoes.

After Mrs T drank her tea she then went to her laundry and looked in the washing machine where fifteen pairs of shoes were slowly turning. 'Ooh I do like shoes,' she giggled to herself. She looked in her sink and there were nine pairs of shoes, and then she looked in her medical cupboard and there seven pairs of shoes. Then she went into the spare room and opened the wardrobe and found a rainbow of shoes all packed together. 'There would have to be at least two hundred shoes in there,' Mrs T whispered to herself.

Now Mrs T was losing hope of finding a spot to put her new shoes so she scuttled into her bedroom still searching for a home to put her shoes. Mrs T looked under her bed and found fourteen pairs of shoes, she looked on top of her wardrobe and found five pairs of shoes. 'Ooh I do like shoes,' Mrs T said to herself with another sigh.

Mrs T was getting stressed now. Mrs T thought and thought about what she could do. Then it struck her — she could have a shoe sale of her own. Mrs T started straight away.

Mrs T painted a sign that said 'Massive shoe sale on now, bargains bargains. Come in now while it lasts.' Then she went around counting and collecting her shoes. She found ... 296 pairs of shoes. Mrs T set up nine benches and laid out all the shoes. Everyone who went past saw an assortment of colours, styles and sizes. Mrs T sold every single pair of shoes — even the ones from her feet.

Mrs T waved the last person goodbye and followed them onto the grass and watched them slowly leave. Mrs T felt the soft green grass under her toes and said in a proud voice, 'I don't want to wear shoes again.'

Mrs T looked up and saw her friend Elizabeth with a very pretty hat.

Mrs T smiled and gave Elizabeth a wave. 'Ooh I like that, I really like that. Ooh I do like hats ...'

2007

The Feeling of Defeat
KARLA PIT

John Curtin College of the Arts
upper secondary category

'G'day, Shelley. Where's ya husband these days?'

'He's just out the back unloading crates. Shouldn't be too long. Can I get you something?'

'Nah, I'm right thanks.'

The pub was filled with the smell of cigarettes and dust, the air thick with floating particles. A small trickle of sunlight seeped through a chip in one of the cloudy windows, somehow illuminating the entire pub. Charlie sat himself on a cold metal stool at the bar, staring at the rustic fan on the ceiling, wondering how the panels had the energy to keep going and going and going ...

'G'day, mate!'

'Oh, g'day, Steve. Sorry, mate, I was just off with the fairies.'

'So I see. The Mrs told me you were here. Hope you didn't make the hour-long journey here just to see my pretty face.'

'Nah, I'm just here to take a look at some cattle. I think I might need a few more cows. The bulls seem to be gettin' a bit restless.'

'Ha, good on 'em! Work must be good, then. So how is it down your way?'

'Yeah, not bad. The farm's holding up pretty good, actually. Can't say the same for this neck of the woods though. Looks like these blokes here are doing it pretty tough.'

'You can say that again. I'll tell ya what; you did the right thing by moving south when you did. Since you've left, it's just gone from bad to worse up 'ere.'

'This drought's a bugger, I'll tell ya that. Puttin' so many good blokes outta work.'

'Yeah, and that's the least of it. You know Jim Baker, the guy that lives near Pete's orchards?'

'The one on Redcliffe Road?'

'That's the one. Took a drive the other day up

Barrier Highway and never came back.'

'No kidding! What happened?'

'Drove his car straight into the Darling. Police say it was just a tragic accident, but we all know he just wanted to put an end to it.'

'Well, I s'pose he felt like he was being defeated. I guess I can see where he's coming from.'

'Too right. Not that I'd have to pull the trigger. The Mrs'd take care of that, no sweat. Speaking of Mrs, how's Jules?'

'Yeah, good. She's in the middle of redecorating the house. Gives her something to do while I'm out in the paddocks all day.'

'Can't have 'em get bored these days, they'll just take you for all you're worth and leave.'

'Well, it's lucky you've still got the farm now you've got another one on the way. At least you don't have to worry about the finances.'

'You can say that again.'

'Yeah, you're a lucky bloke. It's not uncommon for a lady 'round here to do a runner these days. But it's not all doom and gloom, you know. A lot of us still have our families and that's the main thing. Work and money'll come and go but ...'

'Well, I'd better go, mate, if I wanna get home in time for tea.'

'Oh yeah, no worries mate. Listen, I'll see you next time you're up this way.'

'Yeah, no worries.'

As he drove down Silver City Highway, Charlie observed the land on either side of the road. Dead. Nothing but empty tree trunks and burnt blades of grass. He could feel the dejection building up in his bones. He squinted his eyes and looked up at the sky. The midday sun was releasing constant waves of heat that could only be matched by an ocean of lava. Charlie lowered his foot on the accelerator in a bid to outrun the scalding beam, but the further the car sped up the highway, the bigger the sun seemed to swell. Dejection was turning into rage.

As Charlie jumped out of his ute to push open the gates to the dirt road driveway, he stopped to examine his property. Nothing but barren soil. The sight of the bare land made his insides coil. Shaking his head in disgust, he got back in his muddy ute and drove gingerly up the dirt track. He took a left, past the paddocks that once enclosed prized livestock. Now, only decayed carcasses dwelled there, charring under the sun like chunks of coal. Charlie sped up the trail to a refined, timber farmhouse, which looked out of place in its desolate surroundings. He entered the house, giving a tense cough as he cleared his throat. The air was uneasy, and the rooms were hollow and dim. Charlie walked sluggishly up the corridor and peered into one of the rooms. Toys were scattered all over the wooden floor. Crayon drawings were posted on the colourful wardrobe. Its doors were wide open, revealing nothing but empty shelves. The same sensation Charlie felt every time he looked into the room came over him. His heart felt like it was spilling out of his mouth. Instead, he started to weep. He squeezed his face as he tried to restrain the deluge of tears. He took two deep breaths and walked further up the hallway.

In the next room, an ivory-coloured bassinet stood filled with mounds of teddy bears and baby toys. Boxes of furniture remained unopened on the floor, while other pieces of furniture lay partially assembled. Half of the walls were pastel pink, the other half a pallid white. Charlie's stomach twisted painfully as he leant on the doorframe staring at the cot in the centre of the room. Grasping his stomach, he pushed himself off the frame and slowly headed for the front door.

As Charlie climbed into his ute, he gazed at the house, which had once felt like home. He turned on the ignition and drove down to the end of the track, and then onto the main road.

2006

Prima Facie
AMY STEINEPREIS

St Mary's Anglican Girls' School
lower secondary category

A woman wearing galoshes and jangling keys to a 4WD is waiting in the office. 'Tuts' from the secretaries all along the corridor.

'I'm here on behalf of Ned Kelly, who's asking you to act for him.'

Is the lawyer daunted?

'Excuse me. Have you seen my secretary?'

'Which is she?' Gestures to the long line of desks encircling the floor.

'He is Matthew, and you need to make an

appointment. I'm very busy today, so if you would take my card —'

'No time for that. I'm going back to Narrogin tonight. Sunday mass tomorrow. There aren't any lawyers in Narrogin, you know. Ned's been charged with drink-driving.'

'Ned — Ah. Returning to what I said before, I don't have time now. I recommend one of the other lawyers on the floor, we're all part of the same happy family.'

'Your hourly rate is the highest.'

'Indeed, that's because I'm the most experienced. Matthew, please escort this lady to your timetable and either make her an appointment with me or give her to someone who is free.'

Her mobile rings as Matthew and the new client exit.

'Ned calling.'

'Oh, dear. Mr Ned Kelly?'

'Yeah. The drinking and driving.'

'Articulate, exactly what happened, sans adjectives.'

'Yeah?'

'Never mind. Please, continue.'

'Was driving in Subi — I been drinking — was driving in Subi when I turned the corner and the cops are pullin' me up. Get out 'n' them shinin' a bloody light at me. Walk down a bloody side street 'n' they're lookin' at me. Then I'm bein' done for drinkin' and drivin'. Wanted to take me with 'em, but nah ... get back in the car 'n' I went.'

His present tense, imperatives and plurals ... 'Oh, dear. I need a translator.'

'Yeah?'

'The police asked you to come to the station?'

'Yeah, but I wasn't.'

'Did you use physical force against them?'

'Yeah?'

'Did you hit, kick, scratch, bite—'

'Nah, I just get out of there, was all I did. They got the licence plates 'n' they got me later.'

'Excuse me, where are you calling from?'

'The lockup, are youse my lawyer?'

'Oh, dear. I am, yes.'

'Eh, time's almost up. Thanks—'

The line cuts before he can reveal his gratitude. She asks and receives the police report pronto.

Ned Kelly, 21 years, resides in Narrogin WA. Was picked up at 24:03 on Friday 10th May, Barker Rd by Officers Forrest, Dellaqua and O'Kane. Officers noted the driver swerving from side to side of the road and pulled him over. Officers noted that the driver had glazed eyes, slurred speech and

*was unable to walk straight. The driver managed
to re-enter the vehicle while the officers were
extracting their paperwork and drove off. Officers
used the licence plates to find the driver and bring
him to the local station the following morning.*

Coffee break. Her colleague Jeremiah takes it with her. He's young and not a partner yet. She has the upper hand.

'What are you doing?'

'Drink-driver from Narrogin. Changed his name by deed poll, now Ned Kelly.'

'Hmmmm. I'm defending a manslaughter charge! Policeman killed in a brawl.'

'Well done.'

'We're pleading not guilty.'

'Interesting. When's the hearing?'

'Twelfth of August.'

'Is that a weekend? Judge will be Genting, won't it? You don't have a hope. Good luck.'

'Thank you.' He's annoyed.

He leaves her to her coffee addiction and goes to meet his client.

Ronald is a large man. Strong enough to kill a policeman.

'I was with some friends at The Last Stand. We had

a few drinks. I left with Sarah — is she in the police report? — in my friend's car. We went home.'

'That's all?'

'Yes.'

'Would you like to read the police report?'

The other policeman identified Ronald as having been one of two men near the suspect before the time of death. The other man investigated as a suspect, Percival Smith, has a reliable alibi. Witnesses said Officer Grzyb died of stabbing wounds from pieces of broken beer glass. The perpetrator is thought to have exited from the back of the bar, as witnesses do not recall seeing anything unusual before Officer Grzyb went down.

'My friend. Percy was getting drunk. He was getting wild because the cop said he would have to leave. Percy doesn't like cops. His dad died in gaol. I was trying to calm Percy down. He wasn't listening so Sarah and I left.'

'Did Percy leave after you?'

'Must have. I haven't seen him since. He doesn't live here, you know. I suppose he's gone home. But if he's got an alibi—'

Ronald's tone is unnatural, but Jeremiah knows

that's normal. 'Yes, if the police found the alibi to be reliable, your friend will be in the all-clear.'

Jeremiah's client is gone fifteen minutes when a girl walks into the office next door.

'Excuse me. Have you seen my secretary?'

'I'm a friend of ... Ned. The drink-driver?' Her facial features wriggle into position.

'That's all good and well, although you need to make an appointment—'

'—but I don't have time. I'm due somewhere else soon.'

The two women power struggle.

'I was in the car with him when the police caught up with us.'

'There's nothing about you in the police report—'

'People don't see what they're not looking for.'

Oh, dear. The double negatives, she murmurs.

'Ned wasn't drink-driving.'

'He's asked that we plead guilty. According to the police report, there's no doubt—'

'—give it to me.'

'—or would you like me to explain it — no? Here you go.' She adjusts.

Ned's friend peruses it briefly, shakes her head.

'That's what I think. Do you have any reason to believe that Ned wasn't drunk?'

'Hear me. Ned's got pinkeye. Of course his eyes were glazed. They're always red and watery. He's a nervous fellow, he couldn't even get his words out when they asked him his name. And he's got knock-knees. He never walks straight. They picked the wrong fellow to pull over last night.'

'Who are you?'

Ned's friend hesitates. 'Maggie.'

'Maggie? Maggie — I'm afraid what you've said would make it much easier for me to defend Ned. But if Ned wants to plead guilty, we plead guilty. The client has that right, although I can't understand why people do these things.'

Maggie is dismissed.

'Can I help you?'

Sarah appears in front of Jeremiah's workspace shortly after Maggie departs.

'Sarah Smith. You're defending Ronald?'

'Absolutely. He tells me you were with him when the unfortunate incident occurred.'

'We weren't at the bar. We were probably — probably on the road by that time. Ronald and I left Percy with the policeman. They were arguing. The policeman thought that he was in a drunk and disorderly state and wanted to take him outside.'

'Percival Smith has a reliable alibi.'

'Says who?'

'The police, in their report. Would you like me to expla—'

'I'll read it myself, thank you.'

Sarah has a twitch. Not good for a witness who is likely to be put on the stand.

'They don't know that Ronald is guilty. It could have been anyone. It could have been me!'

'There's nothing about you in the police report—'

'I realise that. Perhaps they didn't think a woman was a possible suspect.'

'You'd have to admit that the crime is typically male.'

She is colourless, hanging off his words.

'What is your relationship to Ronald?'

'Friend. Girlfriend.' He examines her response and thumbs through the notes. Scanning the police report, his thought process complete.

'You're Percy's sister? Sarah Smith?'

She starts. 'No. It's a common name.'

'It is. Why were you meeting Percy?'

'He doesn't live here. Did Ronald tell you that? We don't see him very often.'

'Is he antisocial?'

'Look. I don't know. Where is this getting us?'

'Hopefully to the culprit.'

'You said Percy had a reliable—'

'—so I did, but we should always check these things ourselves. Now, if you'd excuse me, I need to organise Ronald's defence, which includes confirming Percy's alibi.'

Coffee break.

'How's your drink-driver?'

'Ned's friend Maggie informs me that Ned is not guilty.'

'Maggie Skillion?'

'The Kelly clan. But Ned wants to put in a guilty plea.'

'Nothing wrong with that. An honest bloke, like the legend.'

'Yes, although with what Maggie has told me I could put up an excellent defence for him. I called back and he's still saying he's guilty.'

'You've got a problem then.' He waits for her to ask how his work's progressing. It never happens.

'Well, I've got news. My client's friend was apparently drunk at the time of death and arguing with the very same policeman just beforehand.'

'There's a lead.'

'Except the police tell me he has a reliable alibi. And he does. He was picked up for drink-driving, of all things.'

'The booze bus caught up with a few of them last night.'

'Obviously. Would you mind helping me with some of the paperwork? Apparently there's been some anomalies with the witnesses' names, one of them misspelled, I imagine.'

'I suppose I can.'

'The police department have just renewed their database and the profile for Percival Smith is no longer showing up.'

He hands her the information and a telephone. 'You'll need to discuss it with the station. Subiaco.'

'Good afternoon. Partner of Jeremiah Stanbrook who is defending Ronald ... Ronald Glendining, manslaughter charge. He says you've called about a mix-up with Percival Smith's name and that his profile is no longer showing on the database. Is that correct?'

'Have you tried different spellings of the name, e.g. Percy, Perce, Percyval, Percivell? Right ... What does that suggest ... Jeremiah, they say he may have changed his name by deed poll ... deed poll? Oh, dear.' She bangs the phone back down on the receiver.

'Jeremiah.'

'Yes. You just hung up on the police.'

'Yes. What's going on here?'

'What's going on here? You were supposed to be

helping me. Now you've just hung up on the police on my behalf. Thank you, thank you.'

'Subiaco police? Changed his name by deed poll? Who does that sound like, Jeremiah?'

'I don't know. My name has always been Jer—'

'My client.'

'Ned Kelly?'

'Yes. We need straight facts. My client and your client are at a bar.'

'My client, your client and Sarah are at a bar.'

'Sarah?'

'Sarah Smith. I thought she was Percival's sister, but she said—'

'Percival's sister? Ned's sister? Maggie! She has a twitch?'

'Yes, although she says she's Ronald's girlfriend, not Percival's sister.'

'They're at a bar. Ned gets into a fight with a policeman. Ronald and Sarah leave. How do they leave?'

'In his friend's car.'

'His friend's car. Percival's car. Ned's car! Ronald and Sarah leave in Ned's car. Ronald is picked up for drink-driving. He doesn't tell the policemen his name because his speech is slurred. They get the licence plates the next day and decide he must have been Ned.

They're the same age. Ned can't speak fluent English even when he's sober.'

'Back to the bar. Ned's getting drunk. He's refusing to leave with the policeman who says he's disturbing the peace. Ronald says Ned doesn't like the police because his father died in gaol. Ned hits the policeman with his beer. He runs, or disappears stealthily. The next day the police catch up with him and charge him with driving under the influence of alcohol. He has the surprise of his life. He realises that if he was picked up for drink-driving he couldn't have killed the policeman at that time. He'll plead guilty. No wonder he wasn't listening when his sister said he had a case. Sarah didn't say otherwise because she couldn't choose between her brother and her boyfriend. Ronald didn't say otherwise because ...'

'Because he thought he might look more suspicious with the additional charge of drink-driving?'

'Possibly. Or was he simply too drunk to remember.'

2005

Shadow Boxing
AVRIL DAVIS

Mindarie Senior College
lower secondary category

The naked bulb glows yellow in the white ceiling. An oat coloured moth flutters around it, wings batting at the hot glass. Sometimes I feel that moth trying to get through to you.

There is nothing to do. The three of us sit around anyway. The scratched varnished tabletop divides us. Ish and Alex face me, sitting in their chairs. They are not looking at me though. Their faces are shadowed and pale under the electric light. A mully bag is dropped on the table, filters and cigarette papers produced and a knife simultaneously fished out of a drawer. There are no scissors.

Outside a car engine idles and we all freeze, Ish poised, knife in his hand. His dad isn't supposed to be home until morning. My eyes skit between Ish and Alex, hands still in my lap. We wait, ears straining, then slowly breathe out. It must have been next door. The drawer slides shut and half the bag of leaf is shaken out onto yesterday's newspaper. Ish checks the open doorframe at the top of the stairs over his shoulder. He sees me looking and smiles guiltily, keep hearing things he mutters. Paranoid I start fiddling with my bracelet. Careful he says to Alex, sitting down. Don't spill any. He sweeps up even the dust. Don't leave anything. I smile at their caution but I smile alone.

Alex and I watch Ish start chopping, knife quick and glinting. The weed is dull and the smell gets up my nose. I twist a strand of hair around my finger, ends bleached blond by salt and sun. Alex says something quietly, something from when he used to smoke weed all the time. Apparently this is not very good quality. He says something about the guy Ish got the weed from too. Who I don't really know. That he's getting stingy. Ish just listens.

It's so quiet I say. Too quiet. It sounds like a complaint. There is no response. They do this a bit — keep me on a tightrope by not answering. I think Alex sometimes tries to prove how much he knows, y'know, wants recognition for his experiences ... but Ish takes him seriously. This good? Ish pauses, sweeping in the pile. I feel excluded. Yeah Alex nods. His hands are big and white on the tabletop, demonstrating a chopping motion. I look up at the moth, still flitting round the light. So futile ... I can't see Ish's eyes, just the shadows of his lashes on his cheeks. Alex's face is pretty much covered by his visor and its shadow. I am slouched on the chair but I can't relax. We feel an edge to me ... with each other ...

The shadows come at me and I never know when, or what they are of. My defences have crept up. I feel like a dancer, on my toes ... Like a boxer with my fists up ... in case the round isn't over. I falter and they offer no indication ...

The curtain rustles slightly at the window behind them. I see our reflections in it, face to face with myself. The light is cold and shallow. My eyes look huge and dark. Alex's shirt is yellow; the same shiny fabric as Ish's but his is red. It's night outside on the balcony. I can see the door between their bowed heads. Alex's voice is low and my attention goes to their conversation. Ish looks up randomly. Stop playing with your hair he says. I drop the twist of hair surprised. Alex starts rolling a joint. Absently I tap the table ...

tuneless. It sounds invasive.

It's Ish's mull but Alex rolls the joint. Ish is still learning that sort of thing. He rubs the back of his head and kind of nods at me across the table. His hair is dark and sticks out in tufts all over his head. Alex is emptying his pockets for a lighter. Ish's foot touches mine under the table and we both pull back. Shit. Where's my lighter gone! Alex's chair scrapes back. A folded piece of paper, thirty cents, a guitar pick and his mobile sit on the table. Gotta find it Ish mutters, moving everything around. They are both up and looking frantically. I cast around the room. Ish overturns the couch cushions, have you looked underneath it? I ask. Hey, it might be outside, Alex goes out onto the balcony and Ish follows. I hear them feeling down the sides of the armchairs, and slap my hand down on the newspaper as the wind lifts it. Some of the mull is blown onto the table and the curtains flap. I knew it was there, Alex is all relief shutting the door behind them. What happened? Ish eyes the mess. You left the door open and the wind ... Clean it up he moves forward cutting me off. Oi Alex, help us clean this shit up. They shove the remaining mull, tobacco, filters and papers in their pockets. Don't light up in here, they'll smell it. Let's go out there. Come on, Ish wipes the table.

I stand up and he picks up the paper. I follow him out onto the balcony. He shakes the paper out into the night. I doubt that it makes a difference but Ish doesn't take unnecessary chances like that. I stand back against the doorframe for him to pass and he chucks the paper back through the doorway onto the table. You're playing with your hair again he says, silhouetted by the light behind him. Alex is already sitting in one of the old armchairs, cherry of his joint glowing neon red. Do you want to sit down? Ish offers me the chair ... nah, it's ok I say, looking over the rail. I sit on the boards and dangle my legs over the edge. The stars look small and far away. I can smell the sea and that distinctive marijuana smoke smell. The ground looks a long way down too. I turn around and sit cross-legged, back against the rail. I can hear the ocean faintly. The screen of his mobile lights Alex's face blue. Let's ring Noah, he says. Inside the moth still battles the light globe. Ish's hair is scruffier in the breeze and he swears as the lighter flame disappears. He hunches, joint held between his lips and shields the lighter with a hand. Finally he gets it lit and sits back inhaling. He blows the smoke at me and smiles, come sit here he says.

Noah leans back and they all belly laugh. We are filling up the night. Or maybe the night got smaller around us. Noah giggles, looks at Ish. You should be

wrecked all the time he tells Ish. Dontcha reckon?
Noah asks Alex. Yeah ... Alex answers. Still doesn't
talk much. Just laughs more, he adds after a second.
Yeah Ish. How come you never talk? Cora demands.
I want to protest that he does talk. He's happy when
he's stoned Alex says unexpectedly. Yeah, you're more
fun when you're stoned Cora states. You're just better
she says. Ish smiles and looks down at his hands. See?!
Noah is triumphant, see? His arm sweeps out in an arc.
Why don't you take up smoking full time? He suggests.
Stay permanently stoned. Cora laughs at the thought.
Go to school stoned she says. He might learn something
I interject. They all laugh. Ooh did you hear that, Noah
crows. She thinks you're dumb Cora taunts. I didn't
mean it I say. Nuh-uh too late says Noah. I no longer
feel secure next to Ish in the chair ...

What would your dad do? Alex asks. Kill me he
answers which we all know except maybe Cora. Ish
isn't always unhappy I don't think. Quietly angry
maybe. What are you pissed off at all the time? Noah
asks. Is it because of Chavelle? He digs. Ish just laughs
and shakes his head. Yeah Cora says. She begins
every sentence like that. Is Chavelle being mean
to you? — What? I look at her. Alex and Noah start
making whipping noises. Stop taking up all the chair,
Noah hisses at me. I smile; If I had a shoe to throw —

Chavelle never wears shoes! Cora launches into a story, Noah and Alex interrupting as she goes.

Cora speaks the loudest, is the bossiest and insults us at random. No one takes it except Ish, who one of us always defends. My fingers drum silently on his knee. Ish slides the bracelet over my hand and puts it on. Cora and Noah spar, poking slapping and even punching each other. Go away, leave me alone Noah yells, arms up shielding his head, but he is laughing too. Alex sips his beer and stubs out the dag end of another joint. I flick my bracelet against Ish's wrist. His veins are thick blue threads running up his forearms under his skin.

Cora starts to sing and we all groan but now and then Alex and I join in. Shut up you can't sing, Noah recommends. Cora sings louder. Spit flies out of her mouth. Good one Noah murmurs Alex. I get up and go inside. There is a stack of CDs near the stereo. All burnt. Except Coolio so I put it on. Ha ha Cora I think. You can't sing to this. I go back outside and we are all quiet for a while. I feel empty. Hollow. Cora starts to complain and I can feel everyone trying not to get annoyed. I'm bored she badgers. Well go I say, not moving. No we won't she looks at me sceptically. I don't want to go she says. I want to do something.

We walk down the driveway into the night. I try to

blend into black but it doesn't work. The night is dusky but transparent. Alex and Noah look like bodyguards. Alex's arms swing and a lit cigarette is passed to Noah. Noah's thongs slap on the concrete. I can't hear my footsteps or my breath. I could almost not be here. The cigarette is returned. I fall behind. Cora bounces around between the boys. The streetlight illuminates them into colour for a few seconds and their words blow back to me. Cora chirps and bosses, Noah teases and Alex banters. They are talking about Ish being stoned. Ish doesn't say anything. He just walks with them. He is thin and fluid in the dark and their voices flow around him.

We should supply him Noah is saying, animated with good intentions. I want to wrap my arms around Ish and protect him from them. And himself. Grass swishes at my legs. I want to hug him and tell him that things will get better. Not to worry about his mum and dad or school or anything. We move through the trees like a line of soldiers. The sky looks lighter peeking out through the branches. Twigs scratch my face but I keep my eyes on the shadowy figures in front of me. Merging, melting and reappearing.

I want to give Ish some happiness to just *be*. I want to put some faith in him so he can have faith in himself. I want to cut his strings and set him free. I figure we are walking Cora home. The streetlights come into sight and the ugly brick estate house houses march along the boulevard. The others are spread out ahead as if we are surrounding something. I watch Ish's long easy strides and I want to trust him, and I tell him that I like him how he is and that I know I am losing him and that I am scared.

Our little group converges on the road ... the conversation has resumed. I am not losing Ish to Cora or Alex or Noah or marijuana or any of that. I don't know what it is. I just feel him slipping through my fingers ... Ish gave me the courage to reach out towards him ... without fear ... and now he just dissolves in my hands.

I tread along someone's front lawn, drifting back to the conversation. Build a massive party bong Alex suggests. And Ish can shout us Noah adds. And us, Cora calls, meaning me and her. We don't smoke Cora I say. No, but we might she replies coyly. I won't I say. That's because you never do anything she says turning to Noah.

I separate a piece of hair, twisting it loosely. Why do you do that? Ish asks. Dunno, I put my hands in my pockets self-consciously. Like a ringlet he says flicking it. Yeah ... Neither of us speaks and we both shift. I am finding this amusing for the wrong reasons. Um, I smile and we both laugh. Ish's teeth are white and he tilts his head, gis a hug he says, arms open. I step into them and hug him. For a moment I hear his heart beat. See you tomorrow I say into him. Yeah. He lets me go and I walk up my steps. It feels like the last goodbye. It feels uneasy. I look back before I go in and he is already gone. His Ishness fading into nothing. Into air. I feel like the moth. Like a shadow boxer.

The Discovery
STEPHEN FARR

Rossmoyne Primary School
middle primary category

It was thirty-eight degrees and Parakeet beach was crowded. In the water a young boy was washing his snorkel gear. He spat into his mask to clean it then he waded deeper and deeper into the cool, crystal, blue water. Placing the snorkel mask into position he lowered his face into the sea and began swimming slowly. A school of large silver fish eyed the strange brown creature but he was not interested in them. They were common in this part. Small bright, electric blue fish darted in and out of the coral. As he snorkelled he saw a pikachu-yellow fish feeding on the reef and he became excited. He swam further into the cave near the limit of his swim without a buddy.

Over the shallow rocks, he swam, diving when he saw two starfish, sticking onto the reef. One was a beautiful blue and the boy reached to touch it gently. It felt bumpy. Suddenly he became excited for there was an orange thing poking out of a small hole in the rock. He watched it move afraid that he might frighten it. It was the most interesting thing he had seen all day, a baby crayfish. It was red, orange colour and it looked like it had been fighting because it had only one claw. It was a great discovery.

All of a sudden he heard people shouting, 'Look! There's a red thing in the water!' The boy looked up. There were two young boys wearing shorts and staring into the water with excited looks on their faces. He remembered seeing them earlier riding their bikes with buckets and fishing nets hanging from their handle bars. Now they were fishing on the reef with those same nets. He panicked. They were going to get it. They were going to eat it. The boy was shocked.

He knew he had to do something and quickly. When they waded into the water and were ready to cast out their nets he dived down like lightning, grabbed the crayfish from the rock, and hid it under his rash vest. Clutching his rashie tightly he swam as fast as he could to the shore and ran to his bike. Immediately he jumped on to the saddle and rode off. On the way he felt guilty, his heart was beating very fast. He knew that he had taken something off the protected reef that wouldn't survive.

When he got to The Barracks where he was staying with his parents, he filled a bucket with salt water and gently put the crayfish inside. He didn't know what to feed it so he gave it some cornflakes. Staring at the crayfish, Alex felt sorry for it. Where was its mother? Was she looking for him like Nemo's dad? After studying it carefully, he decided to call it a name. 'I'm going to call you Claw. What do you think of that Claw? Do you like it? I'm Alex.'

Later when Alex went to play with his friends, he couldn't stop thinking about the crayfish. When he got back he rushed to the bucket and peered into it. The cornflakes now soggy were at the bottom. Claw had not eaten them. His shell seemed a little paler, and he looked unhappy. What had he done? Claw would not survive in a bucket. That night he tossed and turned. Guilt was making him have nightmares. All of a sudden, he woke up then reached for his alarm clock. He knew what he must do. Setting the alarm for 5 am he rolled back into bed and fell into a restless sleep.

The next morning, while it was still dark, Alex crept

secretly from his room with the bucket and carried it to the front door. Carefully, he opened the door so that he would not wake his parents. His mother would have a fit if she knew what he was about to do. He lifted the bucket, and carried it to the front door. When he was outside he placed Claw into his backpack, snuck past the window and made for his bike.

His wheels squeaked as he started the long journey. Faster and faster, he rode whizzing past the dark shapes of trees. He was feeling scared now even with the streetlights on. Ahead he saw small dark bumps like rocks. As he got closer he realised they were only quokkas which hopped out of his way but he nearly hit one. Alex was cycling very fast now. Flying dangerously in fifth gear. Past the little cinema showing *Finding Nemo*. It was getting a little lighter and he became more confident. Past the hotel, past the bakery he rode, further and further towards the beach.

The sea looked very calm but the beach was deserted. It was perfect to snorkel but he still felt fear for he was alone. The most fearful thing of all was in the water, SHARKS! He had heard how they rip their prey up. He also knew that a shark could tear a boat in two with two people inside. He had seen a boat carcass in Cicerello's café. Dawn and dusk were shark feeding time and he didn't want to be main course but he had to return Claw before the fishermen began fishing so he stepped nervously into the water, put on his mask and gently lifted Claw from the dark backpack. The sand felt soft but when he got into the water the shock of cold made him shiver, his teeth chattered but he started swimming towards the reef.

Two stingrays passed him. The reef was full of fish feeding but he wanted out. Lots of fish meant sharks. He was getting closer to the spot where he found Claw. Sea salt was in his mask. He couldn't see for much longer. He went to the surface to empty his mask of water. Then he saw it ... His heart began beating very fast. He panicked. A grey fin was coming towards him. He tried to swim but his mask wasn't on properly. Fear froze his body. He was breathing short breaths until he went under the water. I'm drowning he thought. Help me.

Under the water he opened his eyes as the grey shape brushed him. It wasn't shark teeth he saw but a bottlenose dolphin. He reached to grab its fin and surfaced taking a huge breath of air and gasping. Claw was still in his hand but his mask was at the bottom of the reef. Alex almost laughed with joy, with relief. Filling his lungs with air he took a huge dive down and found his mask on an edge jutting out. Soon Alex had the mask on and was diving down for the last time. Gently Alex set Claw down on the rocky reef and watched him slowly crawl into a safe hiding place. Guilt left Alex now. Happiness almost made him cry. He knew he had done the right thing as he swam away to the shore.

Like My Dad
ISABELLE RIVETTE

St Columba's Primary School
middle primary category

I don't know why I joined the army.

My dad was in the army. I guess I wanted to be a bit like him, even though he left my mother before I was born. He went to war and never came back.

I don't know why I joined the army.

I was only seventeen. I lied about my age. Mum was silent when I told her. She just sat up all night and stared.

I thought it would be great and I was so proud when they gave me my uniform and gun. The lads and I went out that night to celebrate. It was the first time

I'd ever had a drink — a drink? — I had dozens. I spent most of the night throwing up in the gutter. The lads had to carry me back home.

You should have seen the look on my mum's face. She said nothing; but her face — her face.

I'd never hurt Mum before, not like that. I felt so guilty. I didn't know what to say and then it was time to ship out.

We never really got to say a proper goodbye. She just cried and I didn't want to look at her crying, 'cause I would have cried too.

What would the lads have said then?

On the boat over we sang and laughed a lot. Thought we were going to have a great time.

But when we landed, everything was chaos. Next thing I knew I was flat on my belly with bullets flying over my head.

The guy next to me; gosh, I don't even know his name. Well, he got one right in the head. Bits of bone and gore exploded everywhere, I was covered in his blood.

'Move up, move up!' the sergeant shouted.

We crawled forward on our bellies. No time to bury the dead.

We crawled all day, but we only moved a hundred yards further. The ground was soaking, not rain, blood!

I reckon I aged years in that first month. The months and months!

I don't sleep like before. Sometimes I scream out and wake thinking I'm covered in that guy's blood. That guy, I don't even know his name.

I got hit in the leg. Well, at least I got a rest in hospital. They said I was a hero. I don't know why.

I was in hospital two months.

About that time I finally got some mail. It was a letter from my sister back home. She told me Mum had died. How it hurts to think that the last thing I did to Mum was break her heart. I wanted to be a bit like my dad. Well, I succeeded, didn't I?

I don't know why I joined the army.

2002

Frogs in Brown Suits

HEATHER CRAWFORD

John Curtin College of the Arts
upper secondary category

There is a short rap on the door. Not looking up, I
place each of my three pens into my left breast pocket.
Red, blue, black. I rise slowly from the aged wooden
chair, whose creaks of protest remind me daily of its
reluctance to support my weight. The chair belongs to
a set. A groaning chair that matches a splintering pine
desk, set in a painfully bare classroom.

The classroom contains twenty-three odd, smaller
chairs and desks, all of which are arranged into five
rows. Two rows of girls and three rows of boys. A
nice spread. Currently the classroom is empty, school

having ended half an hour ago. Behind me, three sticks of white chalk, issued monthly by the School Board, lie crumbling on a little ledge, just beneath the old school chalkboard. The Depression is upon us and the effects of it are being felt, even here in this dingy classroom. On the chalkboard, a week old heading saying 'Russia' is fading. A furling map of the world establishes the chalkboard's right hand boundary, while a moth eaten American flag, hangs at the board's left edge. The flag of Liberty watches everything that happens, and hears every word spoken in musty classroom 8A, which is located at the end of a streaked brown corridor. A windless flag that has a coin-sized hole in one of its grubby and smudged stars. Two stars across, four stars down. Just left of the centre. Like this town. Just left of civilisation.

I walk unhurriedly towards the knotted timber door. Timing my breathing with each step. Trying to keep control of my excitement. Each paced footstep makes a dull *tick* on the linoleum floor. Each footstep brings him closer to me, and I closer to him. I stop. Only two paces from the door. Another deep breath in. I am very excited. Looking down at my brown woollen suit, I straighten my loose tie, tuck in my thinning white shirt and brush the white flakes of dandruff, from my shoulders. I am nervous too. This is the day I have been planning for months. Each day of each week I have plotted the coming events. In the shower, on my bicycle, in the classroom. Especially in the classroom, where I can't escape him. I have tortured myself with possibilities and with the risks. Being caught would be exciting, but counterproductive. He has tortured me. With those blazing eyes he has tempted me without knowing it. But today he will find out.

He is less than a metre away. He is here after school hours, to help me conduct an *experiment*. An experiment that he wishes to know how to conduct himself. Oh, he'll know all right. I am going to show him how to split a frog's thoracic cavity open, while it is alive. Show him how to keep its heart beating. Pumping blood to organs that rapidly numb from the pain. I will watch his delight, and record it into my memory.

He is *the* biology student. And each lesson his eyes bore through me. Each question that I ask is aimed at him, each answer is forthcoming and sharp. He is thirteen but his knowledge of the natural world is unsurpassed by any of the other students. They are of little matter in any case. During biology, it is just the burning boy and me.

He has, from the very beginning of the year, intrigued me, with his parched school satchel, and pouting mouth. He has one nib-less pencil, which he often uses to carve his skin until it bleeds. He has found his way into my classroom and into my mind.

Occasionally he takes delight in threatening the little girls around him, with a bleeding wound. Sometimes jabbing the plaited cupcakes with his flesh covered pencil. It irritates me when the girls start crying and force me to interrupt his fun. I enjoy seeing pleasure on his face and blood on his body. I don't like having to pretend that I want him to stop. But each biology lesson makes up for each harsh word I have to deal him. His body trembles with enthusiasm. So does mine. His blood caked arm shoots straight up into the air when I ask about a butterfly's life cycle or the breeding habits of a rat. I listen intently. From behind the desk. No thoughts of Policy enter my head, unless I can smell him. When I stand too close or stare too intently, or when I find myself lingering by his side, smelling his wild dirty smell, *then* I am Aware. Aware of the risks. Excited by them. The risks, and his sadness. It can't be wrong. No, we are both playing the same game here anyway. He wants knowledge I want passion, we are doing each other a favour ... whether he knows it or not.

Now he is here. Just outside of the yellowing door. I am burning up. I feel a trickle of sweat slide down my bony spine. I reach out my clammy hand towards the door handle, and hesitate. I check for my pens, Red, blue, black ... I take a firm hold of the cool handle, and with a deep breath, I swing the door inwards.

He is there. Standing there, with those bright sad eyes and droopy mouth. He holds up a large glass jar. For me to see. Inside the jar is a dark green frog, with two black stripes down its back. Large enough to experiment on, not quite old enough to have a family of its own. Perfect. He looks at me. I look at him. I take the jar from him, my finger touching his, just for a second. I look at the frog, and see the reflection of my brown suit on the jar's surface. I smile. It is time to begin. I close the door behind us.

2002

Looking for Yourself
LESLEY EMERY

Perth Modern School
lower secondary category

I looked around and felt the blood rush to my head.

My T-shirt began to slide up my stomach, so I pushed it back down and tucked it into my shorts.

My vision began to blur.

It was strange seeing the world this way and I almost laughed as I watched an upside-down blob of a sausage dog waddle past.

A few seconds later, a pair of Rebox flew by.

I could live like this, I thought, and grinned.

'Eeeewww, GROSS!!' And just like that, my thoughts were shattered and I spun back into reality.

'Your face has gone all purple and puffy,' sneered Bully, my brother. 'Actually ... it's an improvement,' he added in a whisper as he ran away.

I swung myself around, off the tree branch and landed with a thud on the verandah.

The floorboards shook.

It wasn't fair. I was only ten and already I was bigger than both my older brothers.

Mum says I've just matured early, that the boys will shoot up later, that it's just puppy fat.

But I know she's just saying that.

Being heavier than your fourteen year old brother *is* something to worry about.

'Claude,' called Mum from the kitchen. I could hear her banging the pots and pans. 'Dinner time!'

I traipsed inside, my legs itchy and sore from the branch's rough surface.

PLOP! A pea landed in my soup and splashed little droplets all over my shirt.

I looked up to see Bully aiming another one at my nose.

'Mum, Bully's being annoying ... as usual,' I added, scowling at him.

'Stop it Bully,' muttered Mum, not really paying much attention at all.

'Stop it Bully,' he mimicked, spraying crumbs across the table at her.

Mum sighed and asked Dad how his day was.

I hate it when that happens.

Sometimes I just wish that I could be a boy.

My brothers always get away with everything. Especially Bully.

Frankie, the oldest, was born with cystic fibrosis, but in every other way, he is perfect.

Everybody loves Frankie. He has heaps of friends and is the top of his class. Frankie is really musically talented. He plays the trombone, trumpet and cello.

He's going to be famous one day.

Everybody knows it's true.

Two years later came Kevin, a.k.a. Bully. Maybe it was unfortunate that he came into the world with fully functional lungs.

Bully probably made it his business right from the start to try to overshadow Frankie, to direct more attention towards himself, but that only makes him even more annoying.

Is that possible?

Bully has tried all kinds of ways to be noticed.

He once tried the silent treatment and didn't speak for an entire week. He finally cracked when Mum sent him to the Grandparents for the weekend.

He teases people a lot, especially Frankie, but we've got so used to it now and most people just ignore him.

Sometimes Bully deliberately hurts himself, but he really learnt his lesson when one of his cuts became infected and he was sick in hospital for three days. I guess he thought it would be cool, but though he didn't admit it, I knew he hated it in there.

His most famous tactic, though, is to make up these ridiculous stories to try to make people feel sorry for him. At first he was actually successful and people believed his pathetic lies, but then he began to run out of believable ideas. Now people just roll their eyes and say, 'Well, bully for you!'

I'm not sure who it was that first began calling Kevin Bully, but once it was out, the name stuck.

We can't blame Frankie for Bully's attitude though. Nobody could — he's too sweet for that. He's also my best friend.

Two years after Bully came me.

Claudia. The girl. The outcast.

Having two older brothers like mine hasn't been easy.

Nobody except Frankie notices me anyway.

I don't blame them though. I'm nothing special.

I wish I was a boy.

'... Claude ... Claude ... CLAUDIA!'

I shook my head.

Everybody was staring at me from their seats around the table.

Bully snickered. 'She was day dreaming. Again. Who about this time, eh sis? Ooooohh!' He waggled his fingers at me.

'Whatever,' I muttered and left the table.

Frankie was in his room, I could see the light on at the end of the hallway and I could hear him wheezing.

I knocked on the door.

'Hey buddy,' he smiled when he saw me.

'Hi Frankie,' I mumbled.

'Hey, what's wrong?' he asked when he noticed the expression on my face. 'Bully again?'

I nodded. 'He's never really going to change, is he?'

Frankie smiled and patted the spot next to him on the bed. 'Come on. Sing with me.' He took his cello out of it's case.

Frankie and I share a secret. Whenever one of us is upset or angry, Frankie will get out his cello and we'll sing 'Drops of Jupiter', our special song.

I cleared my throat ...

'Tell me did you sail across the sun

Did you make it to the Milky Way to see the lights all faded

And that heaven is overrated

Tell me, did you fall from a shooting star
One without a permanent scar and
Did you miss me while you were looking for yourself
out there.'

'Pow pow pow!' yelled Bully, aiming the channel changer at John Howard's head as if it were a gun.

He swung around to face me and held the remote right up close to my eye.

'Put 'em up or I'll shoot,' he growled.

I rolled my eyes and kept my hands safely on the arms of the chair.

'Bang bang, you're dead. Haha,' Bully giggled and stamped his feet.

I glanced across the room and noticed Frankie playing chess with Dad.

He was a member of the chess club at his school and could easily beat Dad in a game.

I sighed.

Why couldn't Bully be more like Frankie? He really needed to grow up a lot.

Suddenly Frankie had a coughing fit. His arm knocked over the chess board and the pieces scattered across the carpet. Dad banged Frankie's chest desperately and gave Mum a worried look.

'I'm okay,' Frankie grunted. 'Everything's okay.'

I looked back to the TV.

Bully was flicking the channels back and forth.

'There,' *flick*, 'is,' *flick*, 'nothing,' *flick*, 'to,' *flick*, 'watch,' *flick flick*.

'NOTHING!' *flick ... flick ... flick ...*

I closed my eyes and tried to block out the annoying sounds. Bully could be so selfish sometimes. It's as if he doesn't even care what happens to Frankie.

Suddenly the most disgusting smell ever filled my nostrils.

I opened my eyes and, through the blur, saw a great big purple blob.

As my eyes came into focus, I realised the purple blob was part of Bully's shorts and the blob was ...

'Mum!' I squealed, flinging my arms and legs up into the air. 'That *thing* you call a boy just farted in my face.'

Mum glanced over, her mind still on Frankie. 'Be nicer to your sister, Bully.'

Bully grinned and made a rude sign behind her back.

I don't know why I even bother.

I squinted through the thick layer of dust that was forming.

I saw Bully just up the road, kicking dust at his mates.

'... and then she screamed, and it was soooo funny,' I heard him say in a loud voice. He snickered.

The dust began to settle as Bully stopped kicking and sat down on the Rock with the Face.

It's been around for ages, sitting in our front yard, like a bulldog, guarding our house.

I wandered over.

Bully's red lips stretched into a smirk when he saw me.

'Soooo, watcha doing?' I asked, searching for a conversation starter.

'None of your business, Dork Brain,' Bully sneered and his friends grunted.

I think they were laughing at me.

It's the same at school.

I don't have many friends, so lunch time isn't that fun either.

Things were different before Frankie went to high school. He used to let me play with him and his friends.

But now they've all gone and I'm all on my own.

I knew something was wrong as soon as I got home. There was just that feeling in the air.

I opened the door and saw Frankie's bag slung over the back of a chair.

I walked down the hallway and into the kitchen.

That's when I saw Frankie on the floor.

Bully was bending over him.

I screamed and ran across the room. 'What have you done to him?!' I screeched and tried to pull him away from Frankie.

Bully grabbed my wrists firmly and held them together.

'I haven't done anything Claude.' He hissed. 'I found him like this, hear me? I'm trying to *help* him.'

My heart was pounding as I tried to imagine what it would be like without Frankie in my life, having no one to sing with when Bully got on my nerves.

'What ... what happened?' I whimpered.

'I don't know.' Bully sounded worried. 'But we have to get help quickly. You phone for an ambulance.'

I couldn't move — my feet were glued to the floor.

Bully shouted at me, 'Get the phone, NOW!' but his voice seemed to be coming from a million miles away.

The next thing I felt was the sting of Bully's hand across my cheek.

'The phone, Claude. HURRY!'

'Mr and Mrs Baxter?' I heard the doctor say to Mum and Dad.

'Your son is in a very serious condition, but you can see him now, if you wish, in Intensive Care. I suggest that you call a relative or close friend to come and pick up the children. This will be a difficult time for you all.'

'Umm, no. I think Kevin and Claude would prefer to stay here.'

Mum looked at me and I nodded.

'Of course.' The doctor smiled. 'This way please.'

Frankie was lying in bed under stiff white sheets, surrounded by tubes. I could hear the machine monitoring his heartbeat.

Beep ... beep ... beep

I pressed my nose up against the glass and watched as Mum and Dad spoke to him.

Mum leant over the bed and wiped the hair out of his eyes.

It all seemed so unreal to me.

I'd visited Frankie in hospital so many times before, but never like this. Then it had just been routine checkups and treatments. This just didn't feel right.

I remembered what it used to be like — the colourful clowns with their plastic red noses, sparkling eyes and huge smiling mouths and the games room, filled with brightly coloured play equipment, video games and dress ups.

But this time, it was different.

All I noticed was the bleak grey walls, the doctor's

spotless white coat and the purple bags under the nurse's eyes.

Mum and Dad came back through the door and the nurse invited Bully and me inside.

I quietly walked up to Frankie's bed.

I wanted to say something, but my mouth was dry and I felt a lump rise in my throat.

I turned and began to run to the door.

That's when I heard Bully whisper ...

'Tell me, did the wind sweep you off your feet

Did you finally get the chance to dance along the light of day

And head back to the Milky Way

Tell me, did you fall from a shooting star

One without a permanent scar and

Did you miss me while you were looking for yourself out there ...'

Note: 'Drops of Jupiter' song lyrics by Pat Monahan, Charles Colin, Robert S Hotchkiss, James W Stafford and Scott Michael Underwood; © EMI Music Publishing.

2001

School Daze
ALEX MALKOVIC

Highgate Primary School
middle primary category

SIGH! It's 7:30 in the morning and Mum's shaking me awake. 'C'mon Alex it's a school morning,' nags Mum. That's my mum all right. It's all she ever does, nag, nag, nag.

'Aw, all right then.'

'Well I suppose I'll have to iron your clothes, get your toast ready and make your lunch,' says Mum.

'Yeah, well at least I clean my room!' I reply.

'Hardly!' Mum says taking a quick glance at my bedside table, which looks as if a bomb has gone off on it.

'Heh, heh,'

I chuckle nervously, I know what's coming next.

'After school today Alex, you're going to have a big clean-up.'

I groan. It's not like don't try to clean my room, it's just that when I do it, it gets messy again so quickly.

I get out of bed and pour myself some cornflakes. I glance at the toaster and notice that Mum hasn't, even though she said she would, started my toast yet.

Oh well I'll skip toast and have my shower.

Eventually when I'm dressed, teeth brushed, bag packed and hair combed I set off for school But I have to kiss Mum goodbye first. Most ten-year-old boys get embarrassed about kissing their mum good-bye, but not me, I hardly ever get embarrassed.

School is only down the street from us, but the walk goes on and on and on and ...

When I finally get to school every kid's wearing the same boring uniform, so it's not a good idea to go up to your best mate and say: 'l like what you're wearing'.

Our first period is maths, instead of doing my sums, I see how many times I can write 'mathematically boring' in my textbook before recess.

The bell goes for recess. I meet up with my friends, Josh and Tonahtiu. 'Hey guys whassup?' I ask. They groan and mumble something about there's nothing to do.

I agree with them, there isn't anything to do, nothing exciting ever happens at our school but today I have an idea that would brighten everyone's load, well, not the teacher's. I tell my friends my plan. They laugh but agree to help me with it.

We find a stick and go inside to the lost property box. We all peer in and shuffle around rummaging through all the stuff. You wouldn't believe the stuff in there: dolls, shorts, shirts, sweaters and socks.

'Ah-ha!' exclaims Josh.

'I found a pair! Here, give me the stick.'

He bends down and uses the stick to pick up ... a pair of red undies!

'Sweeet!' we all chorus then run outside to the flagpole.

BRIIIIIIIING!!!! The bell rings as soon as we reach the flagpole.

'Great!' says Tonahtiu.

'Now what are we going to do?' asks Josh.

'I'm not keeping them in my bag!' says Tonahtiu.

'Relax guys, I've got it all sorted out, we'll stuff them behind the boys toilet door. No one ever looks there.'

That's exactly what we do.

Our next class is music. Everyone stands up to sing. I don't sing, I mouth the words. The rest of the class drones on and on until finally the bell rings.

'FREEDOM!' our class yells as we run outside. Tonahtiu, Josh and I scoff down our lunch and run to the boys toilet, grab the undies and get to work. Tonahtiu ties the undies to the rope of the flagpole with a piece of string.

'The honour is all yours capt'n,' says Tonahtiu giving me a Swiss army salute.

I pull the rope down, undies go up.

Down, up.

Down, up.

Down, up.

I take a glance at the top of the flagpole and notice that the undies are nearly at the top.

One more yank should do it.

Down, up, KLUNK!

Down up klunk? That's not the rhythm.

Oops it isn't the rhythm. The metal thingy at the top collided with the metal thingy that we hooked the undies on.

We stand up in a line, close our eyes and sing the national anthem while doing a Swiss army salute.

'... *In Joyful strains then let us sing, Advance Australia fair ...*'

'For the school and the nation.'

By the time we've opened our eyes a mini group has formed around us and everyone is laughing. Soon the small group has turned into a huge crowd.

Suddenly the crowd scatters for some reason, little did I know that reason was marching up to us as mad as hell.

'Mrs Lukkhath! Quick men, scatter!' warns Josh.

We all run off in different directions, unfortunately I run in the direction closest to Mrs Lukkhath. Typical.

'Come with me you,' she barks as she grabs my ear.

'OUCH! Hey! That ear's attached ya know!'

'Smart alec eh? I'll show you what we do with smart alecs.'

Smart alecs. It has to be smart Alex. It could've been smart Josh or smart Tonahtiu, but no, it has to be smart alec.

'Sit down and wait,' she says.

I sit in the waiting room while she goes into her office.

The doctors' waiting room is pretty much the same, in both you wait to get treated for.

'Come in!' she hisses.

I gulp, go in and sit down.

'Four weeks' detention!' she snaps.

'BUT—'

'No buts!'

I sit for a second and then burst out laughing.

If only she hadn't used that word.

'Think that's funny eh? You won't be laughing when you get five weeks' detention.'

I groan and leave the room.

FIVE WEEKS LATER ...

Well I've got over my punishment and so has Mum, (though she hit the roof when she found out).

Oh, by the way, at the start of the story I said I hardly ever get embarrassed, check that, I get embarrassed very easily nowadays, especially when I found out the undies were mine.

2000

Seeing through Sticky Tape
JESSICA EDELMAN

Carmel School
lower secondary category

I'm Timothy Marcus Atkinson, but I call myself Tim.
To describe myself in three words, I'm a nerd. I'm not
stupid, actually, I'm one of the smartest kids in my
class. I come top in nearly every test, and I'm always
reading. I'm not even shy! I'm just a nerd.

My brother Danny is the cool type. Cap backwards,
dark sunglasses, you know what I mean. He's always
trying to persuade me to change my appearance.

'Come on Tim, untuck your T-shirt!' he says.

'But my shorts will fall down!'

'Then use a safety pin!'

He complains that my shoelaces are always undone.

Right now, I'm in my classroom, listening to the teacher read us this really interesting book about acid rain and the greenhouse effect. I just can't understand why everyone is yawning and saying it's boring. I'm sitting in between Madeline and Natalie, two giggling girls who relate every subject to what boys they like. It's someone different every week. Of course, I'm never one of them.

'Timothy, would you stop day dreaming! I'm surprised at you! You usually listen very carefully!'

'Oh, um, sorry Miss Frances, but I wasn't day dreaming.'

'Don't be cheeky! And that'll be *Mrs* Frances thank you!'

'Sorry Miss, uh Mrs Frances.'

Then she gives me a 'you better pull your socks up' look.

Mrs Frances isn't a bad person really, for a teacher. Sometimes when we get one hundred percent in a test, she gives us a chocolate frog.

She has two daughters. She constantly boasts about one of them, Amanda, but never mentions the other one.

Mrs Frances is always saying things like: 'Class, you disgust me! You can't even remember the first two lines of *The Pied Piper of Hamelin*, while Amanda knows both 'The Highwayman' and 'The Lady of Shalott' off by heart.'; and, 'How many of you learn an instrument? I think everyone should; you see, Amanda learns the piano and the flute.'; and so on, until we're all so sick of hearing about Amanda, we want to throw up!

'Mrs Frances?' I asked, curiously, one afternoon, 'You never mention your other child. What's she like?'

'Oh, Alison, you mean, well, um, she's very clever too, I suppose. Not as sociable as Amanda though.'

'Timothy! What do you think you're doing?'

'Oh Mum, I forgot to tell you, my glasses broke again, so I'm fixing them with sticky tape.'

'STICKY TAPE!?'

'Yeah, sticky tape.'

'You can't walk around like that; you'll look like a nerd!'

'But I am a nerd Mum.'

'Oh darling,' Mum sighed. 'You mustn't be so negative about yourself.'

'I'm not, I *am* a nerd. I don't care, anyway.'

'Well, if it's because of the clothes I buy you I can always ...'

'No Mum! I'm perfectly happy, okay?'

'Fine, as long as you're happy.'

Mum sighed, and I walked out of the kitchen, and

outside to the basketball hoop that Dad put up last Christmas. Each day I see how many goals I can get in a row. My highest is seven; Danny can get about twelve.

I glanced over to the hoop, Danny was already there, with a bunch of his friends from high school. I couldn't quite recognise them, the sticky tape was blocking my view, but they were all very tall, big and strong.

'Hey shrimp, what are you doing here?' Oh no, he's coming towards me, I better stay calm, not get into any arguments ...

'Oh, that's my brother, Tim.'

'Nice socks mate.'

I suddenly became conscious of my bright purple knee socks, one pulled up, one rolled down.

'Mum?' I asked, when I once again entered the kitchen.

'Yes dear?'

'Why does Danny always get to have friends over? I never do!'

'You never ask me. But sure, you can have friends over if you want to.'

'Thanks Mum.'

I lay down on the couch, and picked up *The Lord of the Rings* which I'd nearly finished.

Then it occurred to me, I had no friends.

No one would want to come over to my house.

The next day I decided to try and hang around some of the other boys in my class. I even played football with them, which I hate. I really don't like sport, I'm always tripping over my shoelaces, and getting teased because I can't catch the ball. I prefer just to sit and read at lunchtime.

But today, I played with them.

'Tim, look out for the ball!'

'Aaaaghh!' I screeched as it came flying towards me. Luckily, Matthew caught it, two inches before it would have collided with my head.

'Hey, sticky tape glasses, do you know how to play?'

'Yes I do. Thank you.' I replied.

'Yes I do, thank you ...' he imitated in a high squeaky voice.

'Hey, nerd, you want to play football, go join those pre-primaries over there!'

Then he swore, as David kicked the ball to him.

I skipped off the field, while nobody was watching me.

That's the last time I play football to make friends.

'I'm home!'

I stumbled through the doorway, tripping over; partly because my shoelaces were undone, and partly because I was having trouble seeing through the sticky tape.

Mum was holding the laundry basket, with a big smile on her face.

'Timothy, I have some fantastic news!'

She put the laundry basket down on the table.

'You remember sitting for that scholarship to Ashbourne Grammar School? I just got the results today, you received the scholarship!'

For a moment I was frozen, I didn't know what to do, I was so happy!

'Wow!' I finally exclaimed.

'I'm so proud of you! How about we go out to dinner, to celebrate; Fast Eddys?'

'Thanks Mum!'

That evening, while I was sitting at a table in Fast Eddys, I suddenly caught sight of Mrs Frances. She was with a very tall man, (her husband I suppose) and two girls.

I immediately recognised the tallest girl from a photograph on my teacher's desk. Yes it was Amanda. She was wearing a flirty black mini skirt, a red velvet jumper and high heels.

The other was wearing a tatty pair of jeans, a bright yellow raincoat over the top, and a pair of glasses.

Glasses — the frames stuck together with sticky tape!!

This was Mrs Frances' other daughter, Alison!

I glanced down at my undone shoelaces, then at hers, and looked up. She was grinning at me and I grinned back.

Mrs Frances was very proud of me for getting the scholarship. She told the whole class the next morning. I also got introduced to both her daughters, Amanda — perfect, beautiful, intelligent (yuck!) Amanda, and Alison. It's a good thing too. Because now, Alison and I are best friends. We have so much in common, we can talk for hours. We don't have to worry about being cool. We're both nerds, both needed friends, and now we have each other.

1999

Wild Riders
LAURA WISNIEWSKI

St Hilda's Anglican School for Girls
upper primary category

We packed our supplies, pulled on our coats, and headed out defiantly to face the wilderness.

We ran screaming down the hillside, and leapt onto our gallant horses in one swift movement. As fearless as could be, we rounded up the sheep, cracking our whips, and chased them to their rightful terrain.

Then through the mighty forest of eucalypts we rode, in and out of the shadows, ever watchful for venomous serpents. We ducked under carefully built snares, and not once were we wrapped in their sticky web. Finally we burst out into the open. Our horses were tired, and we were breathless.

We rested by the great lake, our steeds grateful for its quenching waters. Suddenly the lead horse shied away in fright. We were under attack! We retreated to the safety of the slopes and fought the enemy marron with rock-bombs. They sank back into their muddy world in defeat. Having done our duty, we headed triumphantly back down the hills to the grasslands.

Then we came to unknown territory. We dismounted our horses, and tied them to the trees. Then, as quiet as Aboriginal trackers, we crept down the gully. We were fearless, though we could hear the calls of raptors soaring overhead. Then all was quiet, apart from the crunching of our boots on the dry leaves.

Unexpectedly the path forked!

With no hesitation, we followed the left path, down towards the creek. The valley's sides became steeper and steeper, and the creek swelled. Here, we stopped, pulled off our boots and with the mud squelching between our toes we built a great dam. Our work completed, we stopped to feast on our supplies. We made a fire of brightly coloured autumn leaves, and warmed our hands on the fiery colours.

Storm clouds gathered overhead and the sky darkened. We packed up our camp, marked it with a teatowel flag, and trekked back up the valley. Alas, rain began to fall. We slipped and fell in the mud, and the thunder boomed, and seemed to shake the land. But no, even with our hair plastered down and raindrops racing down our faces, we travelled on.

Behind us the creek rose, and defied our carefully built dam.

We returned to our patient mounts, and, with an Indian warcry, we galloped up the hill, through the storm. Bedraggled and soaked to the bone, our brave and fearless party finally reached home camp.

We unsaddled our trusty horses, and stabled them in the broom cupboard. We soaked gratefully in the warm bath. After being revived with mugs of Mum's steaming hot chocolate, we recounted our adventures,

In front of the real fire ...

With real marshmallows.

I love our farm.

1999

Rory and Albert Find the Yeti

RORY MACLEAN

Scotch College
lower primary category

One day my best friend called Albert came for a sleep
over on my birthday. First thing we did was to argue
about the yeti. So we set our alarm clocks because
we decided to go to Tibet to find if the yeti was true.
The alarm woke us up. I shook Albert up and I said
to Albert it is time and Albert said what is it time for.
I said it's time to find the yeti Albert. We caught the
Fremantle train. It was freezing when we got to the
docks. We went to a burger shop. We had hot chips
and set off to find a ship to take us to Tibet. The man in

the burger shop had told us that there was a ship that was going to Tibet this morning. Albert winked and I smiled. The captain of the yeti ship did not see us sneak on his ship. We found some of the captain's clothes. We put the clothes on and pretended to be sailors. It was a big ship so it was easy to get lost. It took us two days to get to Tibet and now to find the truth. We went to a cafe and we talked to someone who had seen a yeti before. The man pointed the way and said good luck. Albert still said there's no way we will find a yeti. We walked two days and it was getting colder and colder because we were going higher and higher. Albert had never seen snow before. He said it was like cold sand all stuck together. I showed Albert how to make snow balls. We had a snow ball fight and we laughed and laughed then suddenly we heard a noise. We looked up and saw snow falling off the mountain. An avalanche! Albert then saw the yeti. He came out of the snow. He picked us up and saved us from the avalanche and he was eight feet tall and he was all furry. He put us down gently and disappeared. See, I told you Albert there is a yeti. Albert replied, I should have listened to you Rory. Do you think people would believe us Rory? I don't know I said. At least we know the yeti is true. I picked up some snow and rubbed it on Albert's face. Last one down the mountain is a rotten egg. We laughed and laughed while we were rolling down the mountain. What an adventure said Albert. Look Albert the boat is still there I said. We found the captain's clothes and sailed away. We were so tired we slept until we got to Fremantle. The sound of the ship's horn woke us up and the Fremantle train took us home.

What Else Could I Do?
TRACEY CARROLL

Coolbinia Primary School
upper primary category

1. Me + Year 9 + A New School = AAARRRGGHHHHH!

Geez I hate the first day of school, especially at a new school in year nine and the second term. It's a horrible nightmare. It also doesn't help when you're a six foot male with ear length blond hair and ya mum drives ya to school and kisses you goodbye.

BANG!! That's it. I'm trapped in this horse stable of a classroom which is meant to be a home room. I glance quickly through the kids sitting down, they're all staring at me, then I notice there is only one seat left — all the good seats are taken and in the middle of the front row. There is the only seat left gleaming at me saying 'sit here, sit here'.

This little guy walks up to me — well he is small compared to me, he is probably 'bout 5'3". He looks me up and down then glares me in the eyes.

'What's your name sonny?'

'Er ... ah ... um, It's Sam Mcleod.' I say as nervous as.

'Sit down there Samuel,' Here I almost go ballistic, everyone knows how much I hate the name Sam-u-e-l. I go and sit down anyway 'cause I figure he's only just met me and doesn't yet know my feelings. When I sit down my face is bright red so I let my hair flap over my face like two curtains to hide my eyes.

Forty-three minutes of terror and two more left to go. Mr Phelent — I think that is the teacher's name — gave me my timetable but I didn't have time to read it before so I look at it and it seems I have English next. That shouldn't be that bad, I'm pretty good at English if I can concentrate and don't have my friends goofing off around me. I know that won't happen 'cause I don't have any friends here. I mean it's the first day of second term in year nine at a new school, all thanks to my dad's stupid job. Finally the siren has gone, I can survive one more period of this until Lunch 1 — I hope!

It's English, I grab the seat next to the window

in the middle row, 'cause things are normally more interesting outside than in. My English teacher, Miss Martin, walks into the room.

We are learning about punctuation, but it's all stuff I learnt last year so I look out the window, there are these two raccoon-chipmunk kinda things going crazy in the tree outside the window. They get a bit boring after a while when they just go psycho in the tree top. I look around the class again, just as I'm about to look out the window again I see this girl. She is sitting a couple of seats in front of me. She's got wavy brownish-blonde hair half way down her back, it's all I can see of her — but it's beautiful! I spend around fifteen minutes looking at her until I'm interrupted by the siren for Lunch 1.

2: Amanda

Lunch 1 — a time to go to the loo, have a drink and something small to eat — according to the Principal, but fairly I'd like to say: *Yeah Right!* I grab a few bucks out me bag and head to the canteen. I buy a bag of chips and some lollies — that should do me to Lunch 2. I walk around a bit looking for that girl from English. I spot her over by some trees chatting with her friends. I sit on some grass close to her and eat my goodies and pull out me timetable and look at it.

The siren goes again and I'm off to a double period of maths. *BORING!* I see 'the girl' going into the same maths class as me, *YES!* The teacher is Mr Phelent from home room. 'The girl' sits by the window in the second row so I sit right behind her.

I rip off a bit of paper from a sheet in my file, I write 'What's ya name?' on it and nudge her in the back with my ruler. She turns around and I pass the note to her. She takes it and smiles. Next thing I know a piece of paper flies onto my desk, I open it up, it says, 'Amanda! What is yours?' I quickly write back, 'Sam Mcleod.' I then give the paper back.

Time really does fly when you write notes. I might try it a bit more often. Amanda, Amanda, Amanda what a beautiful name. That hour and a half of a maths double period wasn't that bad and now I have Lunch 2 to chat with Amanda.

3: Woodwork

I get me lunch outta my bag and go over to where Amanda is sitting on a bench.

'Can I sit down?'

'Free country.' I sit down and eat my apple while she daintily eats small bites of her sandwich. We start talking and I finally get to *really* hear her voice. We just chat about nothing for the whole of Lunch 2. The siren goes and sadly we have to part. As I walk to put my sandwich in my bag I look at my timetable and it seems I got woodwork next.

Woodwork isn't all that bad sometimes, you can even make some all right things if you actually know how to. It turns out though we can make whatever the hell we feel like. We get a block of wood which is 10 cm x 10 cm x 10 cm. There is not a lot I can really do with it but I end up deciding to make a silly wood heart. I'm almost finished and it doesn't look that half bad. I was about to write 'Amanda' in the middle of it but I just decided I would give it to her instead.

It's after school and I'm looking for Amanda, I can't seem to find her. She must have left already, *shame*. Well, at least I can walk home without Mum coming to pick me up in case Amanda is still here. I'm out the school gates and I've spotted her, she's waiting with her friend, I walk in her direction. She's noticed me, runs towards me just leaving her friend behind.

She's looking at me like something's wrong and her friends are giggling behind her — what is wrong with girls and that annoying giggling? Amanda pulls me to the side.

'Your fly on your jeans is half undone.'

'C**P!'

'Calm down, it's not *that* bad.'

'Yeah well it's not your first day of school or anything.'

'Well it did happen to me on my first day too!'

'Look, I'm sorry. Anyway I've got something for you!'

'Cool! What?'

'This.' I say as I pull the heart from my backpack.

'Thanks!' She says as she runs her hands over my lousy handiwork. She puts the heart in her bag and gives me a kiss on the cheek.

'Bye.' She says as she walks off in the distance to go back to her friends.

All right! Things are starting to look up at this school.

4: Tuesday

I've got a good feeling about today. I'm in home room at the moment and I'm in the back row sitting next to this guy called Jim. He's pretty friendly and definitely weird, well at least the things he claims to do are weird. He said a moment ago that yesterday he brought a dead lizard to school and kept it in the bottom of his bag until he ate it for lunch! I think he is just mental really.

This morning before school one of Amanda's friends Josephine said that Amanda told her to say that Amanda wouldn't be at school 'cause she was picking her brother up from the airport and is spending the day with him 'cause he just came back from travelling around the world and he will only be here for a couple of days, at least it was something like that.

The siren has gone and Jim and I are going to sport together, we are playing basketball. It should be fun! I've always been good at it, probably 'cause of me height or something. Jim is going mental — again — 'cause I dropped my book on the floor and I'm taking forever to pick it up — according to him.

5: Day Three Drama

Wednesday morning 8:25 and looking good. According to my timetable I have home room first with that Mr Phelent teacher person. That shouldn't be so bad, I made one other friend called Jim and he is in my home room so I will try to sit next to him.

Hey there is Amanda, I start running towards her but stop when I see her walking with this other guy around the age of nineteen! That's sick, she is only fourteen, so he is five years older than her, that's gross. And to make it even worse she is now giving him a kiss on the cheek. I thought Amanda and me were like going together, Geez a guy like me really has to learn what's happening or ya'll get in a spot like me. I don't believe her, she could have at least said she wasn't interested in me.

Through all my classes nothing much happened so it's giving me too much time to think about Amanda, Amanda and Amanda. Anyone would think I'm crazy thinking about her after all she has done to me and all, but I keep asking myself why, why did she do this to me? I can't work it out, girls are just so confusing, I don't know what to do.

It's after school and I only now have the guts to ask Amanda what the hell is going on. I'm walking up to her. *I can do it, I can do it.* All right here I go.

'Amanda.'

'Yes?'

'I was wondering ...'

'Wondering what?'

'Well, who that guy was you kissed this morning, I mean I thought we were going together and stuff ...' Then she cracks up laughing, I don't know why.

'He, He was my brother. Didn't Josephine tell you he was coming?' Oh my, I'm such an idiot! I thought he was her boyfriend! I'm such a fool! I don't believe it, I should have trusted her!

'Oh, I'm sorry. I should have trusted you.'

'Don't worry about it it's nothing!' I give her a kiss on the lips mainly 'cause I don't know what else to do and I want her to know how sorry I am.

6: The Break Up

It's horrible, for a month Amanda and I were as happy as the Birds and the Bees together. Then yesterday we had a fight and almost ruined us, even our friendship almost was destroyed. After school it took thirteen phone calls to make her realise how sorry I am. The first six were just wasted on trying to just make her actually talk to me without hanging up the phone.

It wasn't even my fault. I didn't know I was meant to get her silly one month anniversary present. I did give her six of those wood hearts I made in woodwork class and she gave me nothing and I didn't care. Her love was enough for me.

Everything was finally better when my dad told the family during tea that his job was moving him and his family to the US of A. I mean that is so far away from Perth Australia. And it had to happen when things were just about to get good in my life.

It's after school now on Friday and I now have to tell Amanda the news.

'Amanda.'

'That's me name.'

'I gotta tell you something.'

'What?'

'Well my Dad said last night that ...'

'That what?'

'Well he said he got another job in the USA and he took it.' She's lost it she's just started crying and crying she doesn't look like she will stop. What do I do? I sit her down and tell her we can keep in touch through emails, letters and phone calls.

I'm back home and I've already started to pack. I feel like I could start to cry myself at any moment. Life just became ruined — *again!*

1997

The Gift
ERIN MCDONNELL

Rockingham Senior High School
upper secondary category

Leathery wings, tougher than steel, lazily strained against gravity, keeping an eight tonne body effortlessly afloat in the cloudless blue sky. Eyes the size of wagon wheels and the colour of emeralds searched the distant ground for signs of life, be it predator or prey. A snakey tail, pointed like that of the devil, trailed out behind him and the golden scales and precious gems that covered every part of the immense hide sparkled winkingly in the pure, warming light of sunset as the Dragon flew.

He flew fast, very fast. His clear second eyelid

closed tight against the wind rushing past his emerald green eyes. His ears, shaped like a dog's, lay flat against his head as powerful chest muscles pushed him forward through the thin air of clouds and unclimbed mountain tops. He was responding to a summons, a call, that showed a debt needing to be repaid.

The debt had originated many years ago in a clearing, in a forest, beside a desert. The debt was a gift. A knight, his slave and a green-skinned sprite had freely given him this gift, without a challenge and without disappointment. And now the debt was being called in. Unbeknownst to the knight, the Dragon had placed a mark of summoning upon him. In the event that the knight died this privilege of Dragon summons would pass on to his first born child, be it son or daughter. No allowances were made for either sex, both being considered equal in Dragon terms.

As the Dragon pondered this unexpected summons he wondered if the original knight were still living, or if one of his descendants had claimed the call. Dragons paid scant attention to the passing of years. Being immortal definitely dulled their interest in watching the world around them flitter quickly by. Like most Dragons, this one had an impeccable sense of style and would honour his promise to the unsuspecting knight by helping in whatever way he could. As he flew, he thought back to that eventful night when he had met the knight and his two companions.

He had known they were coming to kill him, well try and kill him. He had sent his probing thought out across the desert, marking their progress as they neared the forest, and his lair. He was slightly startled to have his thoughts picked up by the one in the party who was a slave to the knight. Two of the three were dressed in the flowing robes of the desert, but he had easily spotted the red pupils and blue irises of the sprite and the midnight black eyes of the human.

When they had arrived in the forest he watched, unseen, as the knight had unpacked his black armour and the sprite had changed into woodland garb that matched her green skin. He had watched with even greater interest as Takai Floon, the mind reader, dressed in his long, black cloak, had drawn magic circles of defence in the rich soil of the forest floor.

The Dragon could see into the minds of all present, Floon could detect him, so he left Takai alone. He sifted through the memories, thoughts and future hopes of the two he could touch; the sprite, whose name was Vinnet, and the knight, whose name was Kaleb Hawk. He had found both Vinnet and Hawk to be unusual in nature to the rest of their kind. Vinnet had the usual refined sense of prankish sprite humour, but was unlike the rest of her race in that she practised safe jokes, because for some strange reason, she had always found the pranks the rest of her race practised — the ones that killed people — to be distasteful.

Vinnet also cared deeply about the knight, though she had been distrustful when they had first met. Over the five years the two had been companions, Hawk had, without actually being aware he was doing it, won her confidence. The Dragon saw that she would gladly give her life for him and that Kaleb would likewise do the same for her.

He had known from examining their minds that Hawk liked to have a guard posted. The sprite, who had an amazingly potent fear of Dragons, or Draca as she called them, had taken the first watch. The dragon had waited until Hawk and Floon were asleep before he had swept into the clearing on his huge bat-like wings to challenge them.

First, he had frightened them witless, and then watched them closely as he had issued his challenge to them in his deep, rumbling voice. Takai and Vinnet were the slowest to recover from the shock of his loud arrival, Vinnet loosing a harmless crossbow bolt at his golden armoured hide. But it had been the knight who had surprised him the most, with the way in which he recovered his sense. Instead of attacking the knight had begun to cry, not with fear or anger, but with a poet's heart and mind as he realised the full extent of the Dragon's unearthly beauty.

Kaleb's sword had slipped from fingers numb with anguish as he realised that he had been about to kill a magnificent creature, just to prove his worth as a man to others. It was this thought that had touched the Dragon. Not the fact that Hawk would not try to kill him, but that he saw it as an honour to have the chance to choose not to, and from that, see inside to the better part of himself. It was one of the finest compliments the Dragon had ever received, from a mortal.

Now was not the time to be reminiscing. He was nearing his destination and was becoming concerned for the knight's safety. He could only detect the thoughts of a woman going through a painful, lonely labour ... Yes it was her! She was the knight's kin, his granddaughter, and she was giving birth to his great-grandson! The joy of a new life entering the world was enough to stir even a Dragon's heart. As the baby emerged frightened and wailing from its warm, liquid world into the harshness of the Dragon's he let out a roar of pure joy. He circled above the small woodcutter's hut, where a child was breathing its first, drinking its first swallow of milk. No ... wait, the child was still crying and hungry, not warm and happy. The

Dragon suddenly realised that he could not detect the mother's thought anymore.

Shock leapt through him, he was a Dragon! He couldn't fit into the cabin to help the mother, or stop the bleeding he now realised was draining her life away. He roared again, this time in frustration. NO! How could he have come this far only to see his debt unpaid and the knight's only heir die along with its mother! He paused in mid-stroke. The mother was dead. The baby was utterly defenceless and would soon die as well, in its exposed position on the bed.

But wait! There! He had it! It was the only way to repay his debt. What was twenty years to a Dragon anyway? He could only do it once in his lifetime and now was the time! The Dragon felt a peculiar excitement rise within him. If only there was someone to witness his ultimate magic, this amazing gift he was about to offer to a mortal child he knew nothing about.

The Dragon sighed, such was the gift the knight had given him, not only his life, but a decision and an action he could never explain or discuss with anyone else. The Dragon could see it now, it was really the only way to repay the debt in full, and return to the dead knight the honour he had given up for the Dragon.

The Dragon's magic feat took close to an hour to complete and by this time the infant in the hut had ceased its wailing. The Dragon hoped it was asleep. Just imagine giving up twenty years of life, immortal or not, only to find the infant dead. Putting on a brave face, the Dragon drew his cloak tighter about him and stepped through the wooden door of the hut.

The room was still warm from the fire the woman had built before she had gone into her lonely struggle to give birth. The child, who the Dragon now saw to his quiet relief, was asleep, not dead. He walked in and stopped for a second staring at the child's dead mother. Even though she was a granddaughter he could see the faint green shade to her skin, a gift from her grandmother no doubt. He laughed quietly to himself and wondered how long it had taken Vinnet to talk Kaleb into marrying her. If the thought even occurred to her. Sprites were earthy little things sometimes.

He strode across the room to the sleeping child and picked him up. His mother had wrapped him tightly in a warm woolen blanket before succumbing to exhaustion and then dying from blood loss. The child stirred but did not wake as he placed it gently in a rough hewn crib, beside the mother's bed.

With a shovel he found in a trunk beneath the porch, he dug the knight's only kin a deep grave. Placing her in it, he acknowledged the woman's brave sacrifice, but using his dwindling supply of magic to make her a single white rose. Placing the delicate flower in the grave with her tiny form, he worked slowly to cover her over and make a mound of rocks to mark the grave. The boy, whom the Dragon had decided to name Hawk, after his great-grandfather, would always know of his mother's struggle, bringing him into the world alone.

He had finished the sorry job and was contemplating the wisdom of his choice when a fearful wail came from the woodcutter's hut. The Dragon sighed and went inside to comfort and feed his new found responsibility.

Exactly twenty years later:

A lanky lad named Hawk was in despair, the old man had told him not to worry, but he had known Dregon was nearing his final hours. When the old man had finally stopped breathing he had thought he would be able to stand it, but now, looking down at the rough casket that contained his dearest friend and mentor, Hawk could do nothing but weep. Weep, as if his heart had been torn out and left to dangle on the end of a crooked, rusty nail. In the end he couldn't finish the job of burying Dregon, and he had gone inside their tiny hut to make himself a hot cup of tea and maybe have a bite to eat. Perhaps that would fill the aching void inside his chest that seemed bent on crippling him for the rest of his days.

He was seated in his favourite chair when he suddenly heard a splintering crack and a mighty roar that seemed to come from above the hut. Hawk rushed outside to find a huge Dragon seated sedately in his yard, right over the place he had left Dregon.

'Hey! You great oaf! Get off my friend!' He yelled angrily at the Dragon, forgetting to be frightened. The Dragon gave him a bemused look, and fixed one huge, emerald-green eye on the tiny form dancing around in frustration before him.

Hawk noticed distractedly, as he ran up to the Dragon and began shoving uselessly at its scaly hide, to somehow move off what was left of Dregon, that the Dragon's eyes were the exact same shade of green as Dregon's had been. He heard the Dragon laugh softly, well as softly as a Dragon can laugh, and as Hawk put his hands over his ears to drown out the noise, he thought to himself that the Dragon had the same laugh as Dregon too.

Suddenly the Dragon spoke. 'Do you not recognise me boy? I know I look a little different now, but earlier I wasn't feeling like my usual self!' He laughed uproariously as if this was a huge joke, again with his ears covered. Hawk wondered how the Dragon's voice could sound exactly like Dre ... 'DREGON?' Hawk yelled at the Dragon, uncovering his ringing ears, to stare in wonder.

'Dragon, now boy. Dregon no longer,' the Dragon said majestically. Hawk fell heavily onto his rump.

'Dregon?' he said again, this time in wonder, as he looked at the beautiful Dragon claiming to be his dead foster father. The Dragon grinned toothily at the boy that he had raised for twenty years, then he burst into that deep rumbling laughter that Hawk knew so well. Hawk joined in, the Dragon's merriment suddenly catching.

A feeling of freedom flowed from the Dragon like a wave, as he suddenly beat his huge wings and lifted himself into the air, leaving a single thought drifting in the wind behind him.

'You should find yourself a SPRITELY girl and settle down, Hawk!!!!' Followed by a trailing echo of deep, booming laughter. Hawk wondered what the hell he was talking about, probably something about that green girl, Minnet, he met in the forest no doubt. The old man didn't miss a trick. Old *Dragon* now! Hawk corrected himself, and grinned, happily to himself. Maybe he should go and talk to that green girl again ...

1996

Francie's Fear
SIOBHAN DELL

Ardross Primary School
middle primary category

The lunch bell rang. I felt fear and sadness settle in my stomach like a cold stone. How will I make it through another lunchtime without him getting me?

'Hurry up, Francie,' encouraged Miss Hawthorn, my Year 1 teacher. 'You don't want to be late for lunch do you?' I didn't reply because I did want to be late. In fact, I would like to miss lunchtime altogether.

I wandered slowly down to the lunch area and searched for Stephanie. She was in a sheltered corner, sitting on a log. I opened my lunch box and saw two small square vegemite sandwiches and a bag of carrot sticks. I had eaten the biscuit and apple at morning tea so I had already eaten the best things and lunch looked a bit boring.

'I hate lunchtime, Stephanie,' I sighed. Stephanie looked into my lunch box.

'Your lunch isn't really that bad!' she replied.

'It's not my lunch. It's that big boy who will try to grab me after we've eaten. He'll chase me all around the playground,' I grumbled.

'Well, he might not do it today. He does not chase you every day,' replied Stephanie.

'But he might do it today and it's the waiting to see if he does that is so scary!' I declared.

After we had eaten and put our lunch boxes away, Stephanie and I decided to play a pretend game of Mums and Dads with Elizabeth and Harriet. We played on the edge of the playground. Even though the game was fun, I kept a close watch on the Year 7 boys playing basketball. I was sure that any minute now the big boy would race over and try to catch me. I would have to run my fastest if I was going to save my life when that enormous boy in the Hornets cap was after me! It was hard to concentrate on my own game, knowing I might be in great danger soon.

Just when I was pretending to be the baby having a tantrum, it happened! There was a great yell and the huge boy's hands were grabbing at me! I screamed and ran as hard as I could towards the oval. I was frightened and my stomach felt sick. My heart pounded and my mouth was dry. He was bigger than my mum and he howled like a wild animal just behind me.

I pounded straight into Mr McClafferty, the Year 7 teacher. I was so frightened I could not speak even to apologise. I just looked at him.

'What on earth is going on here?' demanded Mr McClafferty. I still could not make my mouth work. My stomach still felt sick and my legs wobbled like jelly.

'I was just playing chasey with this little kid,' laughed the big boy.

Mr McClafferty looked at me carefully.

'Do you enjoy James chasing you?' he asked in a kind voice. I shook my head and tried not to cry.

'You were really scared of James, weren't you?' he asked. I nodded.

'Oh, sir!' protested James, sounding insulted. 'I wouldn't have hurt her. I never hurt little kids, you know that! I just chase one of them every now and then and they like it. They usually laugh and scream all the time.' Mr McClafferty still looked at me and said, 'This one didn't laugh. Didn't you notice? You must have looked like a giant to her and she was very frightened.' I stared at Mr McClafferty. He knew just how I felt!

Mr McClafferty then bent over to speak to me in his gentle voice. 'You're Francie from Year 1, aren't you?'

'Yes,' I replied in a small voice.

'Well, Francie. James wouldn't have hurt you. If he'd really wanted to catch you, he could have done it in about three steps. He just wanted to play a game with you.'

'But he's chased me before!' I blurted out. 'I'm always scared he'll do it again!'

James looked upset and shuffled his feet. 'I wish you'd told me you didn't like it. I didn't mean to scare you like that.' I was amazed! Did he really expect I would stop and tell him anything when I was running for my life away from him?

'You should have told someone,' insisted Mr McClafferty. 'You must never, never go on being frightened day after day. If you can't stop a problem yourself, you must talk to someone who can.'

Suddenly I felt more comfortable inside. The stone of fear and sadness in my stomach just crumbled away. I need never be afraid of James again but better than that I know I can get help if something else is frightening me. I smiled at Mr McClafferty and James and skipped away on happy feet. Lunchtime will be fun again!

1995

Tapestry
EMILY NICOL TSOKOS

St Hilda's Anglican School for Girls
lower secondary category

'No daughter of mine is going to marry into the
Kasidiris family. I'm sorry Maria, it's just not possible.
Your grandmother deserves an apology from those
people and forty years down the track it's just too late.'
That was my mother's response to the announcement
of my engagement to Basil.

'Basil, it's ludicrous. Forty years ago that
Pappadopulous woman embarrassed your grandmother
and I, and she still has not apologised. Maria is a very
nice girl, but I'm sorry — it won't work out.'

That was Basil's mother's reaction to our plan of marriage.

Basil Kasidiris and I had been going out for five years, but strong tension from an ancient family feud still remained between our parents and grandparents. For decades our families had been giving each other the silent treatment over a mystery that had never been explained to Basil or myself.

'Yiayia,' I asked my grandmother in Greek, 'Why does everyone in our family have a major problem with the Kasidiris? I just don't see how what happened was so terrible. It was forty years ago, why have you held a grudge against them for so long?'

My grandmother had been wearing black ever since I could remember. Her hair was silver-grey and always tied in a tight knot at the back of her head. Yiayia's face was creased with lines of age and worry. She never wore any make-up and although she looked over one hundred years old, Yiayia was only sixty-six. Yiayia was a clone of the many Greek aunts, great-aunts, grandmothers and great-grandmothers that I inherited from being a third-generation ethnic.

Yiayia could not speak a word of English, so I had to learn Greek from an early age to communicate with her. Basil's grandmother was exactly the same in every aspect of appearance and personality.

'Maria, those Kasidiris are bad people. Many years ago they disgraced me. Oh, those Kasidiris are very bad ...' Her voice trailed off in a mixture of animosity and resentment. 'Do not be friends with them, they will embarrass you.'

'It's so stupid,' I shouted. 'What do you keep against them? What is it all about? And if it hasn't escaped your attention I have been going out with Basil Kasidiris for five years.'

Yiayia's face went white with shock. 'What do you mean? You said Basil Kasiodopolous! My own granddaughter with a Kasidiris! How can this be? Does your mother know?'

'Yes.'

'Did she let you go somewhere with him?'

'Yes.'

'Do you realise what they did to us?'

'No.'

'Why not?'

'Because you won't tell me. You can't stop me from marrying Basil, but you can tell me what they did that was so awful.'

'Your parents will stop you from marrying a Kasidiris.'

'I'm twenty-four, Yiayia. Legally, I could have married him or anyone six years ago,' I yelled. I stood up and walked towards the door, but then I retreated and calmed myself down. I had a terrible temper. I sat opposite my grandmother and whispered, 'Please, tell me.'

Yiayia sighed and slowly began to open the door of secrets with her words: 'It was the marriage of Aspasia Thalasinos and Andrew Kasidiris. Aspasia was my younger sister's best friend and a very good girl. I remember how much Aspasia was looking forward to the wedding, but of course she had never met Andrew. It wasn't proper for a girl to meet the man she was going to marry before the wedding day. It was all arranged by the father of the family ...'

'Like in *Fiddler on the Roof*?'

'Don't interrupt.'

'Sorry,' I whispered as I looked into Yiayia's sparkling black eyes, reliving the past in her mind.

'Yes Maria, like *Fiddler on the Roof*. Only back then we listened to our fathers, what they said was what we did. Anyway, I asked Aspasia what she would like for a present. She said to me: 'Oh, Mrs Pappadopolous, would you make me a tapestry? You made a beautiful one for Christina Psalos. I would love a tapestry.'

So I made a tapestry for Aspasia, a big bright colorful one with a pattern of two doves holding a wedding ring. I also stitched in a message: 'May God Bring You Years of Health and Happiness.' It was my greatest tapestry yet. Everyone knew me for my tapestry works of art. Then, a few days later, before the wedding day, my cousin had a baby girl. I made another tapestry, but this one had a pattern of a bouquet of flowers with the message: 'Congratulations on Your New Arrival'. Then, on the night before the wedding we have a tradition that all the women go to the bride's parents' house to bless the wedding clothes and the bride. I went to Mrs Thalasinos' house and brought with me one of the tapestries. When the lounge room was crowded with people, Aspasia began to open her presents. She unwrapped the white tissue paper from my tapestry. Her hands were shaking and her dark skin turned a cream colour when she saw the message on the tapestry. One by one, each person came to glare over Aspasia's shoulder to see the insulting words. Everyone gasped, and gossiped quietly. Then, Mrs Thalasinos bolted over and screamed when she read the message. The whole room was silent, Maria. A cold, icy silence and I was the cause of that silence. Aspasia ran away crying and I realised what I had done. I had given the wrong tapestry to her, suggesting that she was pregnant ...'

'Was she pregnant?'

'That is not the point, it's not important.'

'I think it is.'

'Shut up Maria, I'm not finished. No — Aspasia wasn't pregnant but I had disgraced her. No matter how many times I tried to apologise and explain the mix-up, I was ignored and shouted at. Mrs Thalasinos and Aspasia would not listen. I gave up, and refused to attend the wedding. We did not associate with anyone from that family again. I do not forgive them for treating me badly and not accepting my apologies. They disgraced me and my beautiful tapestry,' she complained, wiping the tears of bitterness from her eyes.

'That is so stupid. All that fuss and discrimination over a dumb tapestry,' I yelled at Yiayia. 'My life is going to be disrupted and unhappy because you switched tapestries. I can't believe it. How could you be so stupid?'

'Maria, it was very important in those days. You cannot forgive people who do not forgive you. You cannot forget the past and you cannot marry a Kasidiris,' Yiayia shouted back at me.

'Well I am marrying Basil and you can't stop me,' I said in English, so she wouldn't be able to understand. Our whole conversation had been in Greek as it was every day of our lives. I was so astounded that the whole argument was caused because of a misunderstanding with a tapestry that I rang Basil from Yiayia's house to tell him the details. Basil was more shocked than I was, and we agreed to marry each other despite the warnings from our parents and past.

'Maybe we should have waited a bit longer to get married, Basil,' I said nervously.

Tomorrow was our wedding. After eight short months of constant planning and preparation there was only one night to go before I was Mrs Basil Kasidiris.

Tonight we had invited all of our family and friends to Mum's house where I would receive my wedding presents. Instead of the traditional female gathering, Basil and I decided to invite everyone, ignoring warnings from Yiayia and Mrs Thalasinos.

I was anxious — would Mrs Thalasinos bring up the past? Would Yiayia throw a tantrum? Would they give each other the silent treatment? Or would they forget about the tapestry and act normally? I very much doubted the last option.

After lecturing my mother on how to behave politely to Mrs Kasidiris and Mrs Thalasinos, she agreed to do so, on the condition that they reciprocated. Basil gave his mother the same lecture with a successful result.

The only two people who were victims of the silent fight were Mrs Thalasinos and Yiayia. They were the main cause of my anxiety. After forty years do you forgive and forget?

Time was the only obstacle to knowing the answer to that question, which had plagued my mind for the past eight months. Guests began to arrive and I found myself standing at the front door accepting kind words and gifts. The night was cool and dark, and the black sky glittered with stars.

When I was alone, I stared into the sky watching one big black cloud reveal a glossy white full moon. I gasped with shock — it was an omen, I knew. I began to believe in superstition for a few seconds before I walked inside to face my family, friends and fiancé.

The lounge room was a colourful blur of faces, with the exception of two gloomy black shadows. In one corner sat fifteen old Greek women, wearing black, looking dark and thinking evil — my grandmother's colleagues. In the other corner sat twelve old Greek women, wearing black, looking dark and thinking revenge — Basil's grandmother's colleagues. In between the two cults sat my cousins and friends. Everyone sensed the tension — the room was silent. I looked around for Basil, but I could not find him, so I decided to take action.

'Well, hello everyone,' I said in Greek. 'Basil and I want to thank everyone for coming tonight, but I want to get a misunderstanding sorted out first.'

In detail, I explained Yiayia's accidental mix-up of the tapestries and how she really meant no harm or embarrassment to Mrs Thalasinos or Mrs Kasidiris. Then I told everyone how Mrs Thalasinos would not accept Yiayia's apologies for obvious reasons of temporary anger and humiliation. I said it as though the event had occurred only yesterday, and I had witnessed it too.

'So, maybe after forty years it's time to forgive and forget. Mrs Thalasinos? Yiayia?'

The two old withered women stood up and stumbled towards each other, embracing in a hug and tears of forgiveness pouring out of their eyes. The dark colleagues followed their example and soon the room was alive with rambling Greek conversation. Broken bonds of friendship had been tied together again, and from the corner of my eye I saw my mother hugging Mrs Kasidiris as friends reuniting.

Basil and his friends carried the mounds of presents into the middle of the lounge room, where I began to unwrap them. A flat rectangular package, wrapped in white tissue paper caught my attention and as I peeled off the thin layers of wrapping, I discovered the tapestry. Staring back at me were two doves with a wedding ring in their beaks. The tapestry.

'Maria, it's time to go,' Basil shouted impatiently from the hallway. Our plane was departing in an hour, with the destination being Paris.

'Basil, come in here for a minute,' I called back from the spare room. I was staring at the tapestry, it had captured my interest in a peculiar way.

'What's up?' Basil asked as he entered the small room cluttered with presents in boxes and bags. 'Not the tapestry! Come on Maria, when we come back you can stare at it all you want,' Basil complained.

'Wait,' I said, turning to my husband. 'I just think that it's so strange how our families had been torn apart and their friendships became destroyed. Then, last night we rejoined them, bound them together like a tapestry, like in this tapestry ...'

Basil and I stared at the tapestry — now a symbol of our families united into one. One tapestry tore two families apart, but the same one symbolised them together again. The tapestry of life, each person a small thread which is unimportant unless it is joined with many others. The tapestry. Our tapestry.

When We Were Young
ALAN LAU

Christ Church Grammar School
upper secondary category

I saw her as I was accosted by two giggly young
schoolgirls at the punch bowl. They looked about
fourteen or fifteen, bespectacled and suitably
emaciated. In the usual squirming, breathless fashion,
they asked me if I could autograph their copy of
my book, and I said that I would. I scribbled a little
message, signed it, and they both scampered away,
squealing and clutching their most recent conquest.

She stood on the other side of the room, chatting with
four students from Methodist Boys' School. For a split
second, I thought that I had been mistaken; it had been,

after all, almost twenty years. But it was her all right. There were now tiny lines around her eyes and mouth, and she no longer wore a ponytail, but the fine-boned face remained, and so did the delicate shape of her nose and eyebrows. She now wore her hair shorter, and her suit made her look more sharp and businesslike, but she still looked exquisite and lovely, hence the entourage.

This Young Writers Seminar was my second as a speaker. I had spotted her name on the list of speakers on the first day of the seminar. 'Ms Wong Li Ping' it ran in bold type above the title of her discussion — 'To dig a well'. At first the name did not register — for many years I had kept the memory of her at the back of my mind, letting it grow thick with dust and cobwebs like some old, yellowed newspaper cutting.

I took her in, filling the empty spaces in the hazy mental picture of her that I had carried for almost twenty years. I had almost forgotten how beautiful she was. And then, suddenly, it all came flooding back to me — the kampung years ... when we were young.

Kampungs, or villages, are generally Malay settlements. However, it was not unusual in Malaysia at the time for a kampung to have a predominantly Chinese population as well. My family lived in Kampung Meriah, an hour's drive from Ipoh.

We lived in a typical wooden house built on stilts, or tiang, according to the Malay style. This ingenious development kept us high and dry if the river overflowed its banks as well as safe from snakes and other undesirables that resided in the surrounding forest. In the space under the house we kept chickens and my father's Volkswagen. All around the kampung stood the dense, lush forest, mysterious and earthy-smelling.

Kampung Meriah was a collection of about thirty houses, each occupied by a Chinese family. Master Emeritus Wong, considered to be the kampung spokesman, was the most respected of all the men. He owned the rubber plantation as well as the provision store in town. His house, like the rest, was also on stilts, but it was built of brick and whitewashed. The *tiang* were round cylindrical columns, like the impressive Roman pillars of the Government House in town.

Master Wong was a very large man with a belly that hung over the top of his pants. He had a huge black mole on his right cheek, which, my mother told me, was meant to represent prosperity. I remember wondering how such an ugly thing could bring wealth. If so, the person hadn't really gained much.

We referred to Mrs Wong as Taitai, the respected term for wife. In contrast to her husband, she was skinny and short, and she had a loud, shrill voice with which she gossiped and complained. The Wongs had two sons who were studying overseas, as Wong Taitai never failed to remind us, and a daughter in Ipoh who would soon be joining our school, St Thomas.

'Did you know ah, the other day my Li Ping got her report card. Not one 'B', all 'A's,' she would say. Then, in an attempt to show humility, she would add, 'But also so much trouble. Her prizes fill so many shelves. When she comes home, there will be no place to put them.'

Naturally, I was not convinced I would like this bookworm of a daughter. I had an image of a hideous, disdainful girl with her nose perpetually facing the sky.

Like all my peers in the kampung, I attended St Thomas' Secondary School in town. My father was a clerk at Government House, so he would drive me there in his trusty Volkswagen. On the way, we would pass padi fields, the slender stalks knee-high in water. Sometimes my father would toot his horn, and the sarong-clad women labourers would straighten up and cheerfully wave their straw hats at us.

Town was a different thing altogether. Every inch of it was bustling noise and thick odours. The school was a relic of the thirties, built of stone and peeling paint. In class we sat at battered metal desks tattooed with messages scratched in the paint work. Whenever I felt that what the teacher was saying did not warrant my full attention, I would study them. There was one that read, 'Cikgu (teacher) Hajjiah is a beech'. But one quotation that puzzled me was '*carpe diem*'. It wasn't in the *Pocket Oxford Dictionary*, so I assumed that it had been misspelled beyond recognition. Mr Canning, the big, friendly Englishman who taught us Literature, explained it to me.

'It's Latin for 'seize the day'. That is, to take an opportunity immediately, before it is gone,' he said. Then, with a lewd wink, he added, 'It has its connotations, of course.'

I first saw Li Ping in the school canteen. I had been about to place a spoonful of curry into my mouth when she appeared at the entrance. I remember that very clearly because from the moment I saw her to the moment the bell rang, the spoonful of curry remained suspended centimetres from my lips and grew cold.

The light from one of the windows caught her face as she entered, and for a moment she looked like one of those ancient Greek busts, every feature exquisitely sculptured. Her mouth was half serious, half smiling, like two rosebuds lying gently against each other. For a long while, all conversation at our table ceased as she hesitated in the doorway before joining a queue.

Li Ping became a legend, something everyone wanted to catch a glimpse of, even though she seemed scarcely aware of it. It was as if the boys that gathered in their dozens to gawk at her at recess or after school simply weren't there. I thought she was the classiest girl on the face of the earth.

I started seeing her face everywhere — in the clouds, in the trees, in the shadows of the ripening padi plants, even in my dinner plate. The obscure patterns would rearrange themselves, and there she was. My mother would ask me why I kept staring at my food.

There was no doubt about it — I was hopelessly, entirely in love.

I imagined myself asking her out. At the same time, I was afraid; afraid of being laughed at if I dared to ask. I could almost see it: I would confidently strut up to her and ask, *Would you like to come to the pictures with me?* She would stare in shock, then burst into derisive laughter. *You?* she would say. *Why should I go out with you? You're such a wimp.* And everyone would join in, pointing fingers, and I would try to creep away, burning with shame, wishing I had never been born and ...

The bell rang, saving me from my imagined suicide. Everyone started to pack their schoolbags. She stood up to leave, a rose among thorns.

If only, I thought wistfully.

Carpe diem.

The words seemed to come from nowhere, as if

someone else had spoken them. I was startled. The phrase seemed to ring in my mind.

Don't be silly, I thought. *She's got the best-looking guys chasing after her. She would never ...*

How do you know if you don't try?

I was stumped. It never occurred to me that I would really try. What had Mr Canning said? 'To take an opportunity immediately, before it is gone.' Was this truly my last chance? My mind felt dull and stupid, slow to act.

Before it is gone.

I felt my legs moving. I got up, and suddenly, I was standing before her. My heart thumped wildly, blocking out every other sound. She looked up quizzically. All of a sudden, I realised that this beautiful creature was not even aware of my existence. She did not know my name. Oh dumb, dumb, stupid ...

'Yes, Wei Hong?' Her voice was sweet, melodic. My mouth was suddenly dry, the words stuck in my throat. A faint choking sound emerged.

'Sorry?' Li Ping asked, frowning. 'Could you repeat that?' A cold sweat broke out over my forehead. I could feel my life slipping away.

Carpe diem.

'Would you like to come to the pictures with me?' I heard myself saying. She looked at me (was it shock?).

There was a long silence and I realised that I had made a mistake, a huge mistake. Why was I always so impulsive? I would be laughed out of class, there would be no reason to live, and I would have no choice but to ...

'I would love to,' she said, simply.

We went to watch the latest American release, *Goldfinger*, at the Capitol. I was there half an hour early, wearing a tie and nylon pants. There were no flowers to be picked, so I presented her with two tangerines, moist with sweat from my palms. She accepted them graciously.

I don't remember what the movie was about, I was busy concentrating on sitting up straight and ignoring the intolerable itch from the bug-infested wooden benches. She was watching the movie intensely, unaware of my discomfort. At least she seemed to be enjoying herself, I thought. A million questions ran loose in my mind: What did she think? Did I goof up? What did she think of me? Oh, why did I trip over that step? She probably thinks I'm a nerd ... My palms continued to sweat.

When the ordeal was over, we made our way out of the cinema and I escorted her to her lodgings, a block of flats. When we reached the entrance foyer, she turned to me.

'Thank you for the movie,' she said.

And she smiled.

The world was wonderful, life was wonderful, being alive was wonderful. I rode back on my trusty Raleigh, the metallic squeaks of the ancient wheels sweet music in my ears. Even the padi fields seemed greener that day.

I got her letter in class. It was passed to me by one of her pimply, less radiant friends. It read:

> Dear Wei Hong,
> Please meet me by the Casuarina tree in the playground after school today.
> Wong Li Ping

It was pure poetry. Angels were singing, nymphs and shepherds were dancing over the pastures. When the bell rang, I ran downstairs and hung about the tree for a few minutes before Li Ping appeared. She stopped within a few feet of me.

Being Friday, the playground was deserted. The ancient Casuarina tree spread her wings above me like a canopy. It was the perfect place for two lovers to meet.

'Hello,' I said. She said hello back somewhat tensely. I guess I should have realised that something was wrong, but I didn't.

'There's a new English picture at the Rex,' I said. 'Why don't we ...'

'Wei Hong ... I'm married.'

She said it quietly, but it cut me off like a pail of water thrown in my face. My mind was slow to realise the implications. When it finally hit me, I was stunned. We were standing only a few feet apart, but she suddenly looked small and distant. A gust of wind carried a piece of paper across the playground. We watched it flutter and dance out of sight, no doubt grateful for the distraction. When she resumed, her voice was calm and expressionless.

'My parents married me to my cousin when we were both babies. The fortune-teller told both our parents that we were compatible because I am an earth sheep, and Wu Ching is a metal goat. She said that the combination would produce many grandchildren. When I am seventeen, I must go and live under his roof.' The wind rose up again, and her hair bellowed like a cape. I had never seen her more beautiful.

'I'm sorry, Wei Hong.'

'But ... why?' I managed to croak. 'Why did you go out with me in the first place if you were ...' I couldn't bring myself to say it.

She shook her head in bewilderment. 'I don't know. I really don't. Perhaps it was because I thought that if just once ... if I had a choice ...' Her voice trailed away. 'I'm sorry, Wei Hong,' she repeated. 'I never meant to hurt you.'

We looked at each other for a full minute before she started to walk away. When she reached the school gates, she turned around for a last look, and I saw, even at that distance, that there was pain, and sorrow, in her eyes. And then she was gone.

My senior year in high school passed quickly. I threw myself into my studies, determined to forget everything else. When a school in Singapore offered me a scholarship, I did not hesitate to accept. I wanted to leave everything behind, mainly because there was nothing left.

I wasn't angry at her. I was angry at the system, at tradition that took people's choices away from them. I was sad for her because her life had been written out for her at birth, and now she was forced to spend the rest of her life with a man for whom she had no feelings. She would become part of the system itself, a prisoner.

The students were starting to disappear back into the lecture theatre for their next plenary session. The MBS boys reluctantly left, and she was alone, putting her notes in order. I went up to her.

'Hello, Li Ping.' She looked up. For a moment there was nothing, but slowly recognition crept into her eyes.

'Wei Hong?' she asked cautiously. I nodded, and she gasped. 'My goodness, it's been years!'

'You look wonderful.'

'You look fabulous!'

We chatted about general things. We told each other about our jobs, how the people back home were. She was still very much the shy schoolgirl, conservative but not cold. Eventually, I asked her about Wu Ching, her husband.

'He passed away last year,' she said. She sounded sad. She did come to love him, I realised.

'I'm sorry,' I said awkwardly. 'He must have been ... a very good man.'

'He was,' she said. 'But that's in the past. I've gotten over it. Life goes on, doesn't it? Even if it is the death of a loved one, it's never the end.' She gave a smile, to lessen the tension.

I glanced at my watch. It was almost noon. I was about to ask her to lunch, but I stopped myself in time. I felt a pang of guilt. Wu Ching must have been a pretty decent man for Li Ping to love him. I had no right to intrude or force her hand. The past, the wonderful, terrible past, when we were young ... It was time to let go.

'Would you ...' she began, then stopped.

'Yes?'

She hesitated. 'I was wondering if you would like to have lunch,' she said, and she blushed furiously.

'I would love to,' I said, simply.

The Punished
ANDREW MALCOLM

South Fremantle Senior High School
lower secondary category

The boy ran. Darting through the crowded streets filled with wretched people who eeked out their impoverished existence in a city which did not want them. The boy ran on, attempting to lose the soldiers who chased him through the labyrinth of alleys which filled the poor district. He ran, bare feet pounding against the smooth cobbled streets, his breath coming in short sharp gasps. He had dropped the bread and cheese several streets back and was now running to save his life. Dodging a horse driven carriage, whose driver would not think twice about running over any children in his way, he splashed through the open sewer which flowed along the side of the road. The boy passed children sailing paper boats through the filthy water and a baby, its neck twisted unnaturally, lying face down in a gutter.

He turned down a side alley, an ancient building, several storeys high loomed above him, blocking out the sun. Its impassive, windowless walls were stained black from soot.

The pounding of the soldiers' steel soled boots against the cobble stones of the street and the shrill voice of the captain in pursuit grew ever closer. The boy glanced back along the alley then froze with terror. Soldiers had turned off the street and were running towards him. The boy turned and fled from his pursuers.

'Stop thief!' screamed the captain. 'Don't let him get away.'

The boy could hear the soldiers loading their rifles. Without thinking he dived to his left, towards the coal chute of a building, hit his head on cold hard stone and remembered no more.

The rains had not come at all that year. There was no food or water to be found within the tribe's territory. The dry red dust kicked up by the bare feet of the tribe floated on the light breeze, a sign of their passing. Death would come quickly to those left behind, the old and the young, the weak and the helpless, sacrificed for the good of the tribe. They were moving south-east at an astonishing rate, tens of kilometres fell behind them each day. A young boy, long of leg, with dark black skin and tightly curled hair struggled to match the tribe's pace. He had not eaten more than a mouthful in the last week and was suffering from exhaustion, starvation and dehydration.

'Edward Thomas Milroy. This court has found you guilty of stealing three loaves of bread and two wheels of cheese to the value of sixty pence, upon the 15th of May last. Do you have anything to say for thyself before I pass sentence upon thee?'

Edward glanced up at the pompous judge sitting regally in his imposing high seat. All Edward saw was a tired little old man with big ears. The judge's wrinkled and stained robe, oversized wig and tiny reading glasses which perched on the tip of his nose, combined to give him a conical appearance. Stifling a childish giggle, he shook his head. The judge stared down his nose at him, disapprovingly.

'As an example,' he began in a slow monotone, 'to the thousands of other wretched scum in this city who are, at this very moment no doubt, considering committing crimes similar to yours,' he paused in mid-sentence for breath and effect. 'I hereby sentence you to four years' transportation to the new colony of New South Wales!' The judge finished with a rush then glanced down at the dock to see what effect his words had upon the young offender.

Edward's face contorted into an expression of shock and disbelief and he collapsed against the bars of the dock. A brief smile played across the face of the judge.

The tribe had camped beside the remnants of a permanent waterhole, now little more than a mud bath. All men who were able had been sent to find food whilst the women gathered what edible plants had survived the drought. The boy had been given a spear and sent to find what food might be around. The tribe would be lucky if they could find one wallaby to share.

A fair distance from the waterhole the boy chanced upon a goanna. A large fat goanna, the length of his arm, basking in the sun. It had fallen easy victim to his well thrown spear and now lay on the rock where it had fallen. The boy had been sitting there, dead still for ten minutes, arguing with himself. His immobility belied his inner turmoil. They would never know, he assured his conscience and he would no longer be so horribly hungry. He quickly skinned the animal, spitted it and made a fire. It did not take long to eat the goanna, and, after he was finished he could not remember feeling so full. Contented he lay back against the warm, rough surface of the rock and watched the sun set in a blaze of pink and orange glory, playing with the substantial pile of bones he had made. And that was how they found him.

There were times when he had prayed for death to come and release him from the torture of the voyage. Whatever the Devil had in store for him, down in the bottom-most pit of hell, could not possibly compare to the horrors of the transportation. Chained night and day in their cramped quarters with hundreds of other unfortunate scum, the sickly stench of sweat, blood and faeces, smothering everything like a thick fog. Nine months of sailing aboard the prison ship had changed the boy caught thieving on a street in Old London Town. He was dirty beyond belief and his matted hair, once blond, had grown down well below his shoulders. His face was lined and hardset, masking all signs of emotion. His eyes held a deadly coldness, he had seen more of the world than most others his age and it had not treated him kindly.

'I hear we've been here two weeks,' said the

talkative youth who had been chained next to Edward after the old man had died. Edward raised his head, roused out of his contemplation. He had serious doubts about the boy's sanity, he would not be the first to lose all grip on reality during the endless voyage.

'Some of the boys that been up on deck say we been here for two weeks. Two whole weeks, do you believe that! At anchor, at this New South Wales place.'

Edward ignored him. It might even be true. It was possible that they had finally arrived at their destination, two weeks ago, and had not been unloaded. Edward returned to examining the iron file he had stolen from another convict. The time had not yet come to use it on his bonds, but that hour was growing ever closer.

The shape of the magic man, body painted with abstract designs, loomed up out of the thick smoke. Several fires had been lit and the smoke of green branches rose up into the night air, forming spirit-shapes, dancing in the cold moonlight. The painted faces of the tribe's hunters encircled the boy who lay whimpering on the ground, his eyes rolled back in terror. The tribe's magic man, spirit-like in appearance, bent low over the boy and hissed in his ear.

'Your foolish actions have endangered the tribe and

angered our guardian spirits. What you have done, in this time of need, has threatened the survival of our tribe. It is unforgivable.'

The boy huddled into a ball and closed his eyes, cowering away from the magic man and the power he possessed.

'Stand up boy and take the wrath of the spirits!' the magic man roared. The warriors stepped forward and dragged the struggling boy to his feet.

'With the power of the Earth serpent and the guardian spirits I banish you to the spirit world. You are now dead!'

The gum trees sighed as the breeze rippled through their leaves. Edward sat, watching the sheep he had stolen as they drank from the pool they had found. Above his head a kookaburra laughed, a long ghostly cackle in the sunset. Edward jumped to his feet, reaching for his gun, but could see no one. He was not at ease in this strange new country into which he had escaped. He was wary of the foreign trees and alien animals and he disliked the very land itself. Black men and their ghosts haunted his dreams at night. His waking hours were filled with hunger, thirst and the unforgiving sun which burned down onto the parched landscape. He was however alive and free, free to come and go as he pleased, his own man. He had escaped his imprisonment, was no longer punished.

The boy had been wandering for days now, in a half-conscious delirium. There was no escape for him, he needed no chains or soldiers for his mind. Beliefs formed his prison. During his few sane moments he would eat and drink what could be found and wonder whether he was truly dead. Did he really walk the spirit world? In his fevered hallucinations he saw spirits and walked among them, but he could not be sure.

The sun had risen, the bright young light of morning sparkled on the dew drops covering the grassland. Birds rejoiced in song, sending word of the glorious day ahead. There were no clouds to mar the beauty of the blue sky that stretched from horizon to horizon. The boy sat, his back to a rock, warming himself like the snake. He was happy, happy again, as he had not been for as long as he could remember. For several weeks now he had wandered, unsure whether he was alive or dead, wondering if he truly walked the spirit world. He had been confused, distressed and utterly alone. Today had brought a difference though. He was no longer confused, as he sat atop the rocky outcrop he had seen something which had put his heart at rest.

For, like an answer to his questions, a spirit had come wandering across the plains. His skin was white, like the ancient spirits, and he wielded a spear which brought thunder down from the heavens and could fell a kangaroo in mid flight without being thrown. Most astonishing of all, he drove before him a cluster of clouds. No mortal would have such power, what he saw could only be a spirit. He was dead, he knew that now. He had been punished and now walked the spirit world.

He watched the spirit that day and the next. Making no effort to be quiet or careful as he knew it would be folly to hide from such a powerful spirit. Surprisingly however the great spirit did not seem to notice him, strange too was his apparent unfamiliarity with the land. On the morning of the third day the boy decided to pay a visit to the spirit. He crept down, quietly, keeping his distance from the mystical clouds. When he reached the spirit he looked down at his young alien features, the long blond hair and brilliant white skin. The great spirit was frightening like nothing he had seen before and suddenly he wished that he had never come. With resolution and determination however he sat down beside him and arranged the berries and edible roots which he had brought as a gift.

He waited for a long time whilst the spirit slept

and the sun climbed higher in the sky. Finally the spirit began to stir and the boy leaned forward in anticipation. The great spirit awoke with a sudden start and stared straight into the dark brown eyes of the Aboriginal boy. He yelled out in astonishment.

'Who the hell are you and what do you think you're doing here. You're a blackfella! A bloody blackfella. I'm lucky ya didn't slit my throat right open!'

The boy was surprised and taken aback to hear the spirit jabbering in a strange language, and apparently so frightened of him.

'I am new to the spirit world,' he began, trying to explain. The great white spirit was pointing his thunder spear at him. He had seen the spear before and suddenly frightened for his life he turned to run. He had gone no more than five paces when the heavens exploded with a deafening roar and a bolt of lightening struck him in the centre of the back. Lying on the ground, his lifeblood spilling out in the great gushes he knew he was being punished again by this great spirit, new to the land. As he died one question formed in his mind. Why?

Tim Winton Award for Young Writers

The City of Subiaco established this annual literary award in 1993, with the support of celebrated patron Tim Winton. The award encourages imagination and originality, and provides young writers with an opportunity to develop their writing skills. The award also fosters a love of reading and writing in all Western Australian school students.

For more information about the award,
visit www.subiaco.wa.gov.au

Shaun Tan Award for Young Artists

The City of Subiaco is proud to coordinate this annual visual art award, which is open to all Western Australian school students. Inspired by namesake Shaun Tan, the prestigious youth award has been encouraging creativity and innovation since 2003.

For more information about the award,
visit www.subiaco.wa.gov.au

First published 2013 by
FREMANTLE PRESS
25 Quarry Street, Fremantle, Western Australia 6160
www.fremantlepress.com.au

in association with CITY OF SUBIACO

Cover illustration by Shaun Tan.
Cover design by Ally Crimp.
Printed by Everbest Printing Company, China.

National Library of Australia
Cataloguing-in-publication data is available on request

Government of **Western Australia**
Department of **Culture and the Arts**

Fremantle Press is supported by the State Government
through the Department of Culture and the Arts.